KNIGHT

OF

Paradise Island

Book 6 of the Knights of the Castle Series

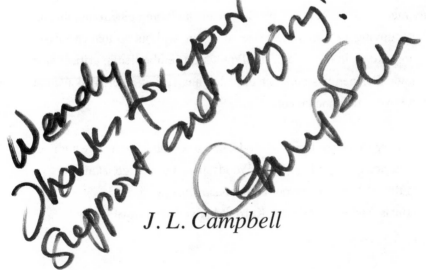

J. L. Campbell

The Writers' Suite
Greater Portmore * St. Catherine
Jamaica

Knight of Paradise Island by J. L. Campbell Copyright ©2020
Ebook: 978-1-952871-04-7
Trade Paperback: 978-976-95586-9-4

The Writers' Suite
Greater Portmore
St. Catherine
Jamaica

Cover Designed by: J.L Woodson: www.woodsoncreativestudio.com
Interior Designed by: Lissa Woodson: www.naleighnakai.com
Editors: Lissa Woodson lissawoodson@aol.com
Betas: Debra J. Mitchell, Kelsie Maxwell, and April Bubb

KNIGHT

OF

Paradise Island

Book 6 of the Knights of the Castle Series

J. L. Campbell

♦ DEDICATION ♦

For those who live with the loss of loved ones, yet find the strength to go on.

♦ ACKNOWLEDGEMENTS ♦

I give thanks always to my Heavenly Father, who provides the creativity that allows me to write these stories. I'm also grateful for my family and the leeway they give me to disappear for hours at a time while I write.

Thanks to Naleighna Kai for conceptualizing and including me in the world of the Kings and Knights of the Castle. Your editing pen keeps me on the straight and narrow.

No book is complete without beta readers and with that said, I'm grateful to Debra Mitchell for her insightful comments and ideas. I'm grateful also to April Bubb and Kelsie Maxwell for their keen eyes and helpful suggestions.

It has been a pleasure working with this group of writers to bring the Knights of the Castle to the world. Karen D. Bradley was gracious enough to let me use her characters and their gizmos.

J. L. Woodson, keep on shining through the excellent work you do with these covers. One day, I will say, "I knew him when …"

The Kings of the Castle Ambassadors, NK Tribe Called Success, and readers in the Naleighna Kai Literary Café are a constant source of encouragement and support. Special mention goes to Brenda Powell Pious, Joyce M. Hudson, Kelsie Maxwell, and Carol Jones, who allowed me to name characters for them.

Thank you.

J. L. Campbell

Chapter 1

Ryan couldn't shake the feeling of being encased in a transparent coffin. The shark cut through the clear, blue water as though coming for him, but it disappeared above their heads. His intuition didn't match the current moment, but he couldn't discount his sense of unease. Every time he ignored his instincts, he landed in trouble.

Aziza threw her head back and grinned over her shoulder, lapping up the experience of tubing through a sealed glass channel inside a giant aquarium filled with some of nature's fiercest aquatic predators. She grabbed his ankles and pointed when the shark's serrated snout entered her line of sight. "Ryan, look."

Her pleasure with everything she experienced delighted him. Ryan loved that about her. Aziza made him view things he took for granted with fresh eyes, which was one of the reasons he was glad he reconnected with her. "I see it, babe."

He wriggled his feet against her side, and she sank her nails in his skin. "Behave."

Laughing, he did the same thing as they slid into an open pool, which signaled the end of the ride. When they left the rubber ring behind, Aziza hugged him as the water cascaded around them. "Thanks for hosting me again. I've loved every minute."

Ryan dropped a kiss on her forehead, then said, "Just returning the favor for showing me your city."

With her hands spread across his back, Aziza scoffed. "You're acting as if you haven't been coming to Evanston since you were a little tiddlywink."

Ryan chuckled. "Whatever that means."

They walked hand in hand onto the sand, and she looked up at him. "Don't forget I knew you when your eyes were where your knees are now."

Ryan threw back his head and laughed. "Says she, who is all of two years younger than I am."

Tugging his hand, Aziza headed for the beach. "Come on, old man."

They sank their feet into the powdery sand, moving toward the one-bedroom bungalow that came with his job at the Paradise Island Grande Resort in the Bahamas. For the last week and a half, they spent most of their nights together in Aziza's room but she had fallen in love with the compact villa that had direct access to the beach via the backyard. Her appreciation for his home confirmed that while she enjoyed the finer things, she also liked the simple life. The house was nice, but not the height of architectural grandeur.

A half-hour after they showered, Aziza sat between his legs. As he combed out her kinky-curly hair and oiled her scalp, Ryan thought how content he was doing that ordinary task. Fact was, he loved touching her. His mother and father hadn't stayed together, but he remembered scenes like these from his early childhood. At some point, his parents had been in love, but life intervened to separate them. He would not allow that to happen with Aziza.

"You have wonderful hands," she mumbled from the patterned carpet.

Ryan leaned sideways on the sofa. "So you've told me a time or two, but don't tell me you're about to fall asleep."

"It's your fault." She yawned and pulled herself upright.

"Hmmm. What are we doing for dinner anyway?"

She tipped her head back on the cushion. "Are you for real? After that lunch, I couldn't eat anything more if I tried."

As he chuckled, Aziza ran her fingers along his leg. "I can't believe our time is over already."

He pulled her hair together and secured it with an elastic band. Then he helped her to sit on his lap and stared into her eyes. "Yes, the days went by so quickly."

Aziza trailed a finger across his chin. "You make a great host."

She hesitated over her next words.

After a gentle peck to her lips, he said, "Speak."

"Have you figured out how what we're doing will work?"

A slow smile curved his lips as he thought about the 18-karat gold diamond ring that grabbed his attention in one of the jewelry stores on the property. Aziza deserved that and more. Next time they were together, he'd ask her if she'd put up with him for the rest of her life and slip it on her finger.

"Everything will fall into place when the time is right," he said. "I have a few things I want to tie down, and you need to finish your contract period in Durabia. Next?"

She sighed and brushed his chin with her lips. "You make it sound so easy."

"Babe, it is. As you well know, this isn't a random, feel-good, love-on-vacation deal. We've known each other too long to end up wasting our time." The assessing light in her eyes made him pause. Then he went all in. "Aziza Hampton, I won't rest until we're in the same place working on all our tomorrows."

She cupped his head between her hands and eased his lips open with hers. Their tongues mated in a slow, sensual dance. Aziza held him close as if hungry for him and as though this was the last time they'd be together so she needed as much of him as she could get.

As his body responded, Ryan relaxed against the seat and let her take the lead. She had his shirt halfway up his chest before she whispered, "Let's take this to the bedroom."

After setting Aziza on her feet, Ryan also stood. "I thought we'd never get there."

Later, they would decide where they saw each other in the flesh next. Now, their bodies cried out for the intimate connection they couldn't do without.

Her phone rang, and she sighed against his chest. "I have to get that."

With both hands resting on her hips, he groaned.

Aziza giggled, then kissed his chin. "It'll only take a few minutes. Most likely, it's Mom checking in with me."

She lifted the cellular off the chair arm and swiped the screen, keeping a hand on his wrist. "Hey, Mom. Why are you … "

He gripped her butt and kissed the tiny frown that marked her forehead.

Aziza's gaze cut to his and concern filled her amber-colored eyes that shifted according to her mood. "What happened to Drake?"

Ryan sat and pulled her down next to him. Her expression went from concerned to frightened as she rubbed one side of her face. As if the air had gone out of her, Aziza slumped when the call ended.

"What's up, Zee?" He slid an arm around her shoulder and drew her close.

She sniffled, then met his gaze. "It's Mom. Drake is in the hospital. His wife isn't sure what happened, but they're running some tests."

"D'you want me to get you a flight out tonight?"

She shook her head. "Mom says he's in good spirits, and he's not in too much pain. No sense shelling out money to change my flight when I'm leaving early tomorrow anyway. You've been so generous already."

The joy of having her with him for two weeks meant he hadn't thought twice about flying her to the island. And he'd be willing to spend more for her peace of mind.

"Let's hope you get some rest tonight," he said, smoothing the frown line on her forehead.

"I'll be fine. They'll let me speak with him when they finish the tests." She snuggled into Ryan's side. "As long as we're together, I can deal with anything. Plus, we don't know when we'll be in the same place again."

"As long as you're sure, I want what you want."

She laid her head on his chest. "After we hear from Drake, we'll make some more memories."

Ryan turned her hand over and kissed her palm. "I'll take every moment with you I can get."

The image of that shark coming toward them flashed in his mind, and a weight settled in his stomach. As he caressed the skin on her arm, he sensed that something other than her brother's health issue was on the horizon.

Chapter 2

"Did you say someone's missing in Durabia?" Ryan walked around the desk and settled into the leather executive chair, moving his phone from one ear to the other. "I'm in the office now and switching over to the chat."

"What are you doing at work on a Sunday morning?" his cousin, Shaz, asked.

"The same reason you're sitting in your office until Camilla drags you away from that desk." He opened the laptop, and Shaz's face appeared on the screen.

"Are you putting on weight or something, cuz? What's Camilla feeding you?"

Shaz snorted. "You're the one who looks like you gained about ten pounds since we last spoke."

"Whatever, man." Ryan snickered because the entire family knew Shaz could eat everybody else under the table. And that meant e-very-bod-y.

"So, back to business," Shaz said. "Aziza is missing."

"Wait a minute, did you say Aziza?"

"You getting hard of hearing, man?" Shaz sounded testy.

Ryan's chest tightened painfully, and he had to clear his throat to speak. "That's not possible."

On Thursday, he spent over two hours on a video chat with Aziza. They ended the call when she started falling asleep over the laptop. The two of them had been following that ritual since she left the Bahamas two weeks ago. She contacted him when she landed in Evanston and again, when she found out her brother was suffering with kidney stones.

The last time he spoke with her was on Friday while she was getting ready to go out with her coworkers. The only reason he hadn't called last night was because of what turned out to be a non-emergency that involved a missing guest. The middle-aged man had turned up disheveled and hung over after a day and night in Nassau. With the eight-hour time difference, he didn't want to disturb Aziza's rest. Now, Ryan knew he should have done so. He'd have been aware of her disappearance earlier.

"Is there something you're not telling me," Shaz asked, his brows elevated.

"Yeah, Aziza and I … let me put it this way. We're a lot more than friends."

Shaz's eyebrows met as he said, "Dang. You've kept that close to your chest, but then you've always been secretive."

"No more than you." Ryan headed him back to the present business, which had his stomach doing drunken somersaults. "When exactly d'you think she went missing and how d'you know that for a fact?"

"Her parents contacted me fifteen minutes ago. Yesterday was Miss Constance's birthday. She and Aziza are close. She said she'd never miss her birthday." Shaz let out a deep breath. "Her mother was in a state after she called the hotel where Aziza works. They told Miss Constance she didn't turn up for work this morning. Her father had to finish up the call with me."

"Does her brother know?"

"His wife just had a baby, plus he's dealing with his own medical issues. Drake can't be out of range at this time."

"Understood."

"There's some other suspicious activity over there that needs our attention. Missing women are involved, so ..." Shaz laced his fingers together and met Ryan's eyes. "I'm asking you to go."

This hadn't been the first time Shaz hinted that he had a special assignment for Ryan, given his five-year stint with the Criminal Investigation Department of the Royal Bahamas Police Force. After reconnecting with Aziza months ago, Ryan had stayed busy with hotel business, as well as expanding the reach of Bostwick Security in the Caribbean. They were in the middle of business negotiations that needed Ryan's input. Now this.

"I figured," he said, sucking in his breath.

Getting away would be challenging, especially since he'd taken time off to be with Aziza. Good thing the director of security at the hotel was his friend. Plus, his brother Myles was more than competent. The two of them ran the security firm and also took on specialized jobs, depending on the needs of their clients.

At thirty-five, Myles was three years older and also in a steady relationship. He was level-headed and wouldn't mind doing double duty while Ryan was out of the country. Ryan's biggest challenge would be those contracts he'd been in the middle of preparing that were yet to be finalized and sent to their lawyers.

"Great. The Kings and I plan to get together within the hour. When we convene at The Castle, we'll set up a video connection to bring you into the meeting."

"Sounds good. In the meantime, I'll talk to Roger Blythe, an extractor who will give me some guidance on navigating through this minefield. He's been everywhere on the map. Then, I'll look at what flights are available."

Shaz nodded and glanced to his left. A smile lightened his serious expression.

"Daddy-Shaz."

His daughter's head popped up behind the desk and a second later, she wriggled between him and the desk and climbed onto his lap. The little girl propped her elbows on the desk and waved at the screen, "Hi, Unca. Where are you?"

"Hey, Ayanna." Ryan wriggled his fingers at the charmer Shaz had adopted when he married her mother. "I'm in the Bahamas."

When he tipped one eyebrow, Shaz chuckled. "When you have a dozen or more uncles, every man other than me gets that tag. Plus, the others travel so much, she understands that screen time means you're not in Wilmette."

As Camilla's distended stomach appeared on screen before the rest of her, Ayanna scrambled to his other side to escape. "Little girl, I'm not playing with you," she said.

"Hey, Camilla."

She focused on the screen, then laid a hand on her belly. "Hey yourself. Everything good?"

Her words brought back the heavy matter Shaz dropped on him. "Yeah, we're fine over here."

"Talk to you later," she said, and guided Ayanna to the floor. "Come baby, let Daddy get back to what he was doing."

Ryan focused on the legal pad where he'd jotted notes for the report he was about to write on the lost-and-found guest. When he looked up, Shaz said, "Don't go anywhere."

Ryan nodded, already planning his next steps. He'd have to advise the hotel that he'd be away, perhaps for an indefinite period.

Chapter 3

"Ahhh."

Some evil person was beating cymbals inside her head.

Aziza struggled to open her eyes, but they refused to cooperate. A man spoke in harsh Arabic, which she hadn't yet learned beyond basic words. Her eyes flicked open when a metal gate clanged nearby. The thunder in her head and the throbbing that came and went in waves wouldn't allow her to focus. The semi darkness didn't help. Where the hell was she?

Someone groaned close by and wailed in a language Aziza had never heard before. She wanted to tell the woman to shut up, but couldn't work up the energy needed. Instead, she kept her eyes closed. The last thing she remembered was feeling a little light-headed and Akbar speaking with her in the corridor leading to the bathrooms at Encounters. After that, her memory failed, coming in snatches—a building here, rough hands there, and feeling nauseous as she did now.

The woman next to her sobbed, and Aziza's attention settled on her. She couldn't be over thirty, but it was hard to tell with the puffy eyes and ravaged features. She wore braids and was model thin.

"What's your name?" Aziza asked, looking at her sideways.

"Naima."

Frowning, Aziza scanned the narrow space. "Where are we? Why are you crying?"

Naima broke into tears again. "You do not understand."

Her words came out muffled as she sobbed into her hands.

Impatient, Aziza raised her arm to push the hair out of her face. That's when she realized someone had shackled her to a pallet covered by a flimsy mattress. Other women surrounded them, their wide eyes conveying varying degrees of fright. Aside from that common feature, all of them wore identical hospital gowns. A second look confirmed they were house dresses with buttons down the front. Aziza wanted to drop someone. Who had dared to treat her like a rag doll and remove her clothes? And to replace her dress with the ugly dishrag she now wore? She needed answers.

"We are prisoners," Naima said, sniffling.

Aziza sat up too fast, and put a hand to her head. When the room stopped wobbling, she turned to the other woman. "Did you say we're prisoners?"

She nodded as her eyes filled again. With one end of the scarf covering her braids, she dried her tears. "They captured me yesterday. When I got here, you were unconscious."

Either the woman was on drugs, or Aziza had woken up in a horror movie. The handcuff that kept her tethered to the bed said this was her reality. But what happened between happy hour at the club and this moment was a mystery.

Around them, other women groaned as they woke. The sounds of despair and misery escalated. As far as Aziza could tell, at least twenty women were confined in the space. The metal walls around them told her they were inside a double-wide container, which grew hotter by the moment. Ventilation was almost non-existent, but she took comfort in the fact that an air-conditioning unit sat on metal brackets high above them. With the rising heat, she swore she inhaled the women's fear into her nostrils, but this was no time to be afraid. The hum of the cooling unit starting up brought relief.

Then clanging noises came from the far end of the container, and she craned her neck.

The lights came on and two men, each wearing a *keffiyeh*, or head covering, stood in the doorway. The material also shielded their faces. Only their eyes were visible. The stouter of the two carried a gun and locked the door when they stepped inside. From this distance, Aziza couldn't see his eyes to gauge his temperament. The second man was slight in build and carried a tray with foil boxes she assumed contained food. He placed one on each bed as his companion watched with a keen gaze. When he reached the back end of the unit, Aziza threw a glance toward the entrance and asked in English, "Can you tell me what day it is?"

She figured today was Saturday or Sunday, but needed to know for sure. Also, she wanted to be certain whether he spoke English.

He looked at her, his eyes black as midnight, but didn't act as if he understood her words.

"'Ayn nahn." Where are we? She asked in Arabic.

Surprise flickered in his gaze, and he turned his head to where the other man stood. The moment he opened his mouth, the gunman took heavy steps toward them. He spoke in rapid-fire Arabic, which went over Aziza's head. When he glared at her, she knew he'd heard her words.

He pointed the rifle at her and growled. "Kun hadyaan."

Aziza understood that he was telling her to shut up, and didn't need him to say it twice. She was deeply disturbed by everything happening around her. Panicking, in fact. Why had they imprisoned her when she had committed no crime?

Chapter 4

"You have all the information Shaz provided." Ryan's gaze settled on the man across from him at the tiny café table. "What else can you tell me?"

Bashir Farooq, one of the Sheikh Kamran's trusted assistants, laid an envelope on the tabletop. "This details Miss Hampton's movements up to the time she disappeared."

"How did you collect this data?" Ryan asked, opening the sealed envelope and scanning the sheets that outlined Aziza's daily routine.

The aide squared his shoulders under his expensive jacket. "My position gives me access to information that wouldn't be available to ordinary men."

Ryan considered that, then tipped his head to one side, "Thank you. Give me a minute to go over it."

The bearded, olive-skinned man nodded once and sipped from the cup of black coffee he'd ordered.

Ryan glanced at his watch, impatient to meet with the hotel security, but Roger Blythe, the extraction expert, advised against what he called knocking at the front door of the establishment. She had been housed in a residential unit owned by the hotel and if her disappearance potentially involved anyone on staff, Ryan needed a subtle plan of action rather than raising an immediate alarm. Roger's mention of "human trafficking" had made Ryan's blood run cold.

He wanted Roger to accompany him, but he'd just gotten married and was in the Bahamas on his honeymoon. Shaz enlisted the help of the Kings—his brothers who managed The Castle, a philanthropic organization in Wilmette, a far north suburb of Chicago—and they agreed he would travel directly to Durabia and investigate, then make contact from there. He expected at least two or three of them to arrive within days. The rest would follow later, if needed. He hoped that wouldn't be the case.

"Are you sure you're up for doing this?" Shaz had asked on Sunday.
"I won't be able to rest if I don't."

The pictures he'd revealed of a young African-American woman with her belly slit open deeply disturbed Ryan and he refused to consider, even for one moment, that Aziza would have that kind of luck. The graphic display made the trip more urgent.

After his talk with Shaz, he had a meeting with Myles to cover important contract points. They also planned to have Ryan attend meetings online, as necessary.

He boarded a plane on Sunday evening and landed in Durabia seventeen hours later. Arriving when he did, meant he could go straight to work.

Myles would say that without sleep, Ryan was running on fumes. The job sometimes meant going for days with little to no shut-eye. He had tonight to rest. Now, he had a mission.

The ring in his luggage was a reminder of his mother's favorite expression. Never put off for tomorrow what you can do today. He'd done exactly that with Aziza, and now he was paying the price.

He raised his head from the sheets of paper to find Bashir watching him over the rim of his cup. Ryan didn't yet know what to make of him. He had watchful eyes and didn't speak much. They were evenly matched in terms of height and physique. As far as Ryan was concerned, anyone who gained his trust had to earn it. For all he knew, Bashir was assigned to him to be in a position to cover up anything the authorities in Durabia didn't want made public.

As he sifted his thoughts, he swallowed a mouthful of coffee. Laying the papers on the table, he said, "Thanks for your help. If I need anything, I'll contact you later today. I'm going to check in and get a few winks."

Ryan stood and waited for Bashir to do the same. When he did, they shook hands. The micro expressions that crossed his face revealed that Bashir expected to be with him longer than an hour. He wasn't discounting any help the man could give, but he'd handle today's business on his own.

He wheeled his suitcase to the entrance of the alcove that served the café and crossed the marble tiles in the elegant lobby. At reception he checked in for five nights, hoping he'd wouldn't need to lengthen his stay. The longer he took to find Aziza, the more unlikely it was that he'd get her back alive.

Inside his room, he pulled the curtain aside. The stretch of blue sky was endless and the sand below, dotted by lounge chairs and vacationers. And yet, inside he was empty. The inability to pinpoint Aziza's location, plus not knowing what condition she was in, left him reeling. This minute, he didn't have the words to voice a prayer.

He turned away from the modern skyscrapers in the distance, opened his suitcase, and unpacked in ten minutes. He didn't intend to get comfortable. Ryan simply couldn't stand looking untidy, even in casual wear. Another glance at his watch confirmed it was time to be downstairs, back in the café he left minutes ago. He stored the laptop but took an iPad with him.

The moment he entered La Palma, he spotted the first person he needed to interrogate. She wore jeans with a tank top and sat with her chin propped on her hand. As he slid into the seat opposite her, she leaned away from the table as if startled. "Deirdre?"

She nodded while studying him with curiosity shining from her eyes. "Ryan?"

"Yes, thanks for meeting me."

They shook hands. She quickly withdrew hers and sat back in the seat, studying him.

"How did you get my cell number?" she asked, letting her gaze slide to the Bahari Bahamas logo on his t-shirt.

"It's not a secret. Information is always readily available." He smiled to put her at ease. "You simply have to know how to find it."

Deirdre didn't look away from him, but the tense set of her shoulders spoke volumes.

Ryan offered a reassuring smile. "I understand you were one of the last persons to see Aziza before she disappeared."

After sucking one side of her lip into her mouth, Deirdre nodded. "Yes, we went out on Friday evening. For happy hour."

"Is this something you did regularly?"

"Me? Yes." With one finger, she brushed the hair off her forehead. "Aziza mostly kept to herself. She'd go out with the rest of us maybe once each month."

That was in line with what Aziza had shared with him. Deirdre was also telling the truth. The dossier Bashir provided included dates, times, and photos of the persons thought to be involved in her disappearance. He wasn't yet looking at Julene, the woman with whom Aziza shared the apartment. He'd already been in touch with her and was satisfied that she knew nothing more than she'd already told him. They had spoken several times during his Skype sessions with Aziza, and his instincts told him Julene was a decent human being. Also, Aziza liked her and that was good enough for him.

A waiter came to take their order, and Deirdre declined to have anything. Ryan settled on a cheese croissant and bottled water.

"Are there many Americans working in this hotel?" he asked when the man walked away.

She shook her head and the sleek bob danced, then settled around her mahogany skin. "Maybe ten of us, including Aziza." She leaned across the table and spoke in a hushed tone. "Are you here to investigate what happened to her?"

"I'm here to find her."

Laughter intruded on their conversation. Several groups of businessmen sat at other tables.

She sighed and focused on her hands, which trembled. "I hope you do. Aziza is good people."

Frowning, Ryan asked. "Do you know if the hotel is doing anything about locating her?"

Deirdre shrugged. "They've questioned all of us who went out that evening, and they've searched her apartment and questioned Julene, who also lives there. I'm also sure they must have reported her missing."

"Do you know that for a fact?"

She nibbled on a thumbnail, then met his gaze. "If they thought she left on her own, then they might not try too hard to find her. But she was on contract, so she wouldn't up and leave without notice."

"Were the police called in to investigate?"

"The police interviewed us earlier today, but you might want to check out that place we went for happy hour. It's legit, but you never know." Her gaze shifted when she added, "Some of these men are always trying to pick up Black girls and that's how some go missing."

Ryan's eyebrows gathered in a frown. "Some?"

Deirdre glanced around them, then at her watch. "Surely you don't think Aziza is the first of our kind to disappear. It is a problem here, which is why the hotel tells us to always travel with company. In pairs, at least. It's not stated as a warning, more as cautionary advice."

The waiter returned with Ryan's order, which he moved to one side. "Is there anyone in particular you think I should talk with at Encounters?"

She stared through the glass at the tourists going past, then looked directly at him. "Try the bartenders. They know everything, even if they try to tell you otherwise. Also Akbar, who's employed here, might be able to tell you something. He works at reception, and he's thick with the barmen."

Shifting sideways on the seat, Deirdre said, "I have to go now. I'm on duty in an hour."

"Thanks for talking to me."

She smiled as she stood. "I'm glad someone's looking for Aziza."

Ryan bit into the croissant and followed her with his eyes as she exited the café. He made a mental note to find out more about Deirdre before the day was out. She was saying all the right things, but her energy was off, as his mother would say.

Chapter 5

The clanging of the lock warned them of the men's approach before they appeared. Either they were back with more substandard food or they were coming for other nefarious reasons.

In halting English, Naima, who turned out to be Senegalese, told Aziza she was sure they would all be trafficked. Aziza had tried to make sense of her situation as she followed the sequence of events that brought her to the present moment.

Naima turned frightened eyes on her. "Don't say anything," she pleaded. "That way they might pass over us."

In the doorway, their jailors stood in front of a tall, bearded man wearing a cream linen tunic. His authority was obvious as the other two nearly fell over themselves to get out of his way. Strolling, he went past the row of cots, coming closer to the back of the container. He pointed to one woman, then stopped a foot from where Aziza lay and pointed at an East Indian girl. She was little more than a child and shrank into a ball, sobbing.

The stout jailer shook his head and pointed to the entrance. As they jabbered back and forth, Aziza gathered that they were encouraging the man to take one of the other girls, who were closer to the front. From the looks of it, they had some kind of system.

When their jailor wouldn't give in to the visitor, he stomped his foot and strode back the way he came. The door banged shut behind them, and the women breathed a collective sigh, then whispered to each other.

Earlier in the day, another visitor came. He brought two others with him, and they dragged two girls screaming from the container. Their cries chilled Aziza's soul, and when the man she assumed was a buyer backhanded them across their cheeks, she wanted to get in his face. But what could she do while shackled like a slave?

As the day wore on she felt a tad better, but needed water, which seemed to be rationed. She ignored the food they provided but drank the bottled water when she couldn't hold out any longer. Thankfully, it didn't make her feel any worse. She wasn't sure how many hours had passed since she regained consciousness. Someone had taken the watch Ryan gave her on her birthday. Her handbag, containing her phone and keys, was also missing.

At the thought of Ryan, her eyes smarted. Did he know what happened to her? And if he did, would he come halfway around the world to find her? A cloud of depression threatened to swamp her, but she kicked her chin into the air, then sat up. "Aye!"

"Are you crazy?" Naima whispered, her eyes round and red from her tears.

"Aye!" This time, Aziza banged on the wall behind her. She continued until the door opened and Hamid, the young jailor, stepped inside. He frowned and glanced over his shoulder at the gunman, who sent a glare in Aziza's direction.

"What you want?" His words surprised her because she'd assumed he didn't speak English.

"Bathroom. I need to use it again."

He turned toward his partner, and they threw words back and forth until he sailed a set of keys through the air, which Hamid caught with one hand. He uncuffed Aziza and helped her stand.

The gunman pointed his rifle at her and though she didn't understand what he said, his intent was clear. He'd shoot Aziza if she made any wrong moves.

She walked ahead of Hamid to a door a few feet away. He opened it, and they entered another container equipped with bathroom facilities. A toilet, basin, and shower occupied the clustered space. She faced the door and met Hamid's gaze. "I'm not using the toilet with you watching."

Aziza pushed the door, but Hamid slid his toe in the opening.

She yanked the flimsy, wooden panel toward her. "You better not spy on me while I'm in here."

His foot stayed in the doorway, which didn't leave her any choice but to do her business with him in earshot. Same as last time. As she washed her hands, the reality of her situation hit, and she scanned the small space for anything that might help her in a crisis. The primitive shower rail wouldn't do her any good, but when her gaze landed on a curtain hook, Aziza smiled.

She unhooked one of the metal clips from the middle, hiked up her dress, and slid it into the side of her underwear. Thank goodness they hadn't stripped her to the bone. She grabbed a bit of tissue, then moved back into Hamid's line of sight to dry her hands. The dirt in the bottom of the shower stall told her it wasn't used regularly, so with luck they wouldn't notice anything amiss.

Aziza stepped past Hamid to the sound of the other jailor grousing. He eyed her from top to bottom, as if he suspected her of something. He barked angry words to Hamid, then as if to make a point, rammed her in the back. Pain lanced through her spine and buckled her knees. She held on to the wall until the agony subsided. When she stood straight, she glared at her attacker. "Does it make you feel good to beat up a woman?"

He snarled and raised the rifle. When the butt connected with her face, pain splintered outward from her jaw, and she crumpled to the floor.

Chapter 6

Vikkas Maharaj, international lawyer and Shaz's fellow director of The Castle, frowned at the police chief. "You still haven't told us exactly what you have done about finding Miss Hampton, and we've been sitting here for a half-hour already."

Someone rapped on the door and entered the room, when invited to do so. The man did not wear a uniform and from his aura, Ryan assumed he had some authority. He nodded toward the visitors, his gaze sweeping over them, then addressed the Assistant Commissioner in Arabic.

They exchanged several sentences, while the visitor stroked his mustache. In another minute, he withdrew from the office, carrying a file the portly officer handed to him.

Durabia's top law officer was slender to the point of emaciation. Ryan guessed his sleek, black hair had been styled by a professional. The Commissioner shot a glance at his second-in-command, the physical opposite of himself. After clearing his throat, he said, "The case only came to our attention on Sunday."

"And today is Wednesday." Vikkas lifted the thin file he'd received and let it fall to the desk. "The size of this tells me nobody has done anything to find Miss Hampton."

"Things are not the way they look." The police deputy protested, raising thick hands with stubby fingers. His gaze slid to a thicker file on the marble desk. "There are other cases that demand our attention."

Ryan pointed to the file at the deputy's elbow. "Do they relate to the same thing?"

"Well, if you mean—"

"You still haven't told us anything that can help us find the woman we're seeking." He looked sideways at Bashir, who accompanied them thanks to Sheikh Kamran's generosity. "If you can't help us, then maybe we have to take things from a different angle."

The police chief frowned. "What do you mean?"

Ryan let his gaze rest on the expensive African Blackwood desk, the sleek furnishings that he'd never seen in any police station anywhere else, and finally, the heavy folder on the desktop that he suspected would help their investigation. "The fact is, you are stone-walling us."

When the two officers frowned, he added. "You are messing us around, yanking our chain, putting up roadblocks, obfuscating."

With each word, Ryan's voice grew louder. "The longer you pussyfoot around, the less chance we have of finding Miss Hampton." He stabbed the edge of the desk with one finger. "Now, we need your cooperation, and we need it fast."

The Assistant Commissioner blustered, sitting taller in his seat. "It is not proper protocol for you to force our hand in an investigation—"

"On which you've done nothing."

Vikkas gripped Ryan's arm, which stalled his outburst. The man's calm demeanor and silent message were clear. *Let me handle this.*

"What Mr. Bostwick is trying to say is that we will achieve what we came here for … one way or another." Vikkas released Ryan's arm. "It's up to you how we carry out our mission."

Ryan drew a calming breath. "Let me put it to you this way. Your Sheikh has been kind enough to help us, and you are blocking the process. I wonder what he'd have to say about that. I'm thinking he'll want to know what interest you have in standing in the way of us finding this woman."

Now, the two shared a concerned look and again, the stout man's attention went to the thick folder on the desk.

"Does the information in that file include data on other women who have gone missing in Durabia?"

The two officials eyeballed each other again, but neither answered the question.

"These cases are of a different nature," the chief supplied.

"How different?" Ryan asked.

"Sir, that is not information you need," the Assistant Commission spat.

"If I may ask," Vikkas said, "What percentage of women who go missing in Durabia are found?"

"Five percent," Ryan supplied through his teeth.

His research netted him that information. He was sure his blood pressure would skyrocket if the fools in front of him didn't stop wasting his time. While he was sitting in an air-conditioned office being fed a load of bull, his woman was somewhere in Durabia, being kept under God knew what conditions. At the thought of what she might be going through, Ryan wanted to grab the scrawny man across the desk and choke the air out of him.

Vikkas sighed, a reflection of Ryan's impatience. With his fingers steepled under his chin, Vikkas said, "The fact is, if you do not provide us with the information we need, we can always get it in a way you will not like. Things can be clean and clear-cut ... "

"Or they can be uncomfortable and messy. You decide." Ryan raised his brows, waiting for the officers' response. "I think there's a simple way to resolve this issue."

Every man in the room focused on Ryan. A slow smile spread over his face as he said, "I'm very short on patience, especially when someone's life is at risk. So here's the deal. Since you're refusing to give us what we need, we must find another way to uncover exactly what happened to the woman we're trying to find. The international media is always looking to pick up news items, especially human interest stories." He waited a moment before adding, "In places that have a reputation for condoning atrocities against women."

The Commissioner's eyes bulged as he flung a panicked look at his deputy.

Ryan lowered his voice, so they had to strain to hear him. "I'm not sure how you would deal with having media houses calling you at all hours of the day. And how would it look to have news teams pouring into Durabia to report on the American woman who's missing. And from the look of things, others have gone before. Maybe think about that for a bit."

"And there is something else." Bashir inclined his head toward Ryan and Vikkas. "You need to consider what you will say when it's time to explain to Sheikh Kamran why you did not show these men every courtesy that could be extended by the Durabian Constabulary Force."

Chapter 7

"So, your agent just gave you up once you got here?" Aziza asked, frowning.

The Senegalese woman sighed, and her eyes filled with tears. She shifted onto her side to face Aziza. "I thought the modeling agency knew about the trip to Durabia. We were already in the air when confirmation came that it was something he arranged to benefit himself. I did model in the show, but how could I have known he planned to sell me into slavery when it was over?"

More tears escaped from her eyes, making Aziza blink hard. The reality of their situation settled deeper in her soul with every hour that passed. A grapefruit-sized lump blocked her throat, and it was a moment before she controlled her emotions. Crying wouldn't help them, nor would wallowing in their misery.

In the four days since her capture, several girls and women disappeared in ones and twos each time their jailors visited. Aziza's stomach somersaulted at the image of the hideous, frog-like man who ran his pudgy hand over her leg a day ago. She rubbed her calf where he cruelly wrung her flesh just because he could. The kick she flung at him by reflex earned her another whack across the head from the man she now knew as Abdul.

Naima's intense stare brought Aziza back to the conversation. "This girl isn't cut out to be anybody's slave, so we have to find a way to escape."

"It is impossible," Naima declared, sniveling into her headscarf, while her braids spread around her like a black tide on the dirty sheet.

"So you plan to go quietly with them when they sell you to some fat sheikh who will abuse you?"

"We do not have options," she said in a monotone.

"Yes, we do."

When Naima lifted her head off the cot, Aziza continued, "We just don't know what they are as yet."

"And time is not on our side." Despair filled Naima's voice, and she waved at the empty beds.

The women who originally occupied them had vanished, and Aziza estimated that their time would come in another day or two. They didn't have the luxury of lying around acting like damsels in distress.

When the sound of metal grating together reached them, Aziza's heart pumped hard. So far, they had been fortunate the men who came wanted young girls. The ones interested in them had cruel eyes, which confirmed they were masochists, who wanted them as playthings rather than as sexual partners. Only eleven females remained in the beds coming down to theirs. Thankfully, they were teenagers. A pang of shame hit Aziza for hoping other women would suffer instead of her.

Her gaze shot to the entrance, where the door creaked open. The effect was eerie and prolonged, like something from a horror movie. When only Abdul and Hamid appeared, she sighed. No buyers this time. Hamid flicked the light switch, bathing the back of the container with light.

Carefully balancing the tray he carried, Hamid distributed the soupy mess of bread and vegetables. At meal time, Aziza forced down a portion of the cold, unappetizing glop to keep up her strength. They left all the lights on while they ate, and Aziza studied the other women. She didn't have to worry about Naima. She was docile and would do what she was told, if it helped her situation. The youngest of them was a thin, East

Indian girl with matted hair and huge eyes.

The others were a mixture of races—Black, Caucasian, Indian, and Middle Eastern.

"Hey," Aziza called. "Do any of you speak English?"

At least five of them nodded. She scooted to the side of the cot to get closer. "We need a plan to get out of here. Who's with me?"

One woman shrank away, but after a whispered exchange with the female in the next bed, they both nodded and sat straighter.

"Who else?" Aziza asked.

A few hands went up, and the women's eyes lit with hope. A small girl huddled on the cot nearest to the doorway continued sobbing. Her misery pulled at Aziza, but she couldn't afford the distraction. If they were going to get out of this container, they needed a strategy and they needed it fast. She motioned for them to come closer and whispered as loudly as she could so they all heard what action she thought could work.

Naima frowned at the food in her container, then said, "So, for now, you want to use some kind of diversion, but after that how are we going to get out of here? What about when we are outside?"

"I don't have all the answers. If we can disarm Abdul, that will be a first step, don't you think?"

An ominous squeaking from the direction of the door signaled that they had company. The women's head swung in that direction, their default reaction. Abdul and Hamid appeared, and the prisoners' relief was palpable. This time, none of them were destined for parts unknown.

Abdul studied each female, his eyes dark with suspicion. When his attention turned to her, Aziza willed herself to drop her gaze. Challenging him wouldn't win her any favors, plus her face was still stiff from yesterday's blow. If he'd used any more force, he would have dislocated her jaw.

While in a haze of pain, she'd been aware of someone picking her up and laying her on the cot. She mumbled and grabbed hold of his clothing, but he gently disengaged her fingers while harsh commands in Arabic rang in her ears.

When she raised her head, Abdul was still staring at her. Aziza told herself to relax. He couldn't see inside her mind. His gaze shifted to Naima, and her blood chilled.

The lust in his eyes was unmistakable.

She hid her disgust, praying he wouldn't act on his base nature. He looked like a man who wouldn't deny himself anything he wanted. Abdul couldn't seem to make himself look away. His intensity made Aziza's insipid lunch almost come back in the wrong direction.

He pointed to Hamid, then motioned to Naima.

Aziza exchanged a worried glance with Naima as her stomach plummeted.

Chapter 8

The cool air-conditioning was exactly what Ryan needed to de-stress, never mind that he was still on Aziza's trail. He now sat inside Encounters with Bashir. Although it was the middle of the week, the place was hopping. The décor looked like something out of an IKEA store, and the crowd included a mixture of races, which wasn't surprising. Durabia's capital city was a metropolis that attracted people from all corners of the world. The standard of living was good, and professionals came in droves, seeking opportunities to advance their life goals.

"I think I'm turning into an old man," Ryan muttered. "This crowd is unreal."

Beside him, Bashir sipped from a bottle of water while he scanned the lower level of the club. "And it is like this most days of the week."

Across from him, Alejandro Reyes—called Dro by his fellow Kings—tapped a finger against his glass of soda water. "It's a jungle."

He, too, focused on the floor below them. Ryan was interested in one of the bartenders, Jahani Bahar. After interviewing the man Aziza's coworker mentioned, Ryan was unsettled. Akbar seemed to be open and honest, but there was something about his eyes. He wouldn't look at Ryan for more than a few seconds at a time.

Shaz had asked Dro, the crisis management expert on the board of the Kings of the Castle, to make the trip to Durabia a priority. If anyone could bring some clarity to the situation, this man would. That was the assurance Shaz provided. Daron, a security and technological expert, would follow in another twenty-four hours.

Dro had landed an hour ago. They had a secure tele-conference on his way from the airport and agreed to meet and survey the activities at Encounters. If this was where Aziza disappeared, then it stood to reason that she wouldn't have been the first or last woman to fall victim to whatever scam was in play.

A disturbance below pulled Ryan from his thoughts. A Black woman got up from her seat at a table with two young men, who looked like natives. She spat some words at them, then with her drink in hand, she marched to another seat a few feet away.

The men she left behind sat with their heads together, deep in conversation. After a moment, they gestured to the bartender, Jahani, then looked in her direction. He nodded once, and by the time Ryan focused on her again, another man stood at her table. He took the seat when she waved a hand toward an empty chair.

"What has you so interested?" Dro asked, training his dark-brown eyes in the same direction.

Bashir's gaze followed, and he leaned forward to see better.

"I'm not sure if it's something or nothing, but that woman left these two guys over here." Ryan pointed with his chin to where the men watched the same female as if they were security personnel. "And no sooner does she land than another man is homing in on her. Almost like it's a setup."

"Why the suspicion?" Despite the doubtful note in Dro's voice, he hadn't taken his attention off the woman, who shot to her feet. She stumbled and put a hand to her head before moving away from the table.

The man followed.

Ryan and Dro exchanged a knowing look and stood at the same time.

"What do you need me to do?" Bashir asked, getting to his feet.

"Watch the bartender," Ryan said over his shoulder as they headed downstairs. "If he moves, you're his shadow."

On the ground floor, Ryan made a beeline for the woman, who was unsteady on her feet but continued moving toward the entrance.

"I'll watch her," Ryan said, leaning toward Dro to be heard over the latest Rihanna release.

"Those two knuckleheads are mine." Dro's dimples flashed in a sharkish grin.

Ryan followed the woman dressed in a snug wraparound dress, but kept his distance to see if his suspicions would play out as expected.

She left the club and walked across the sidewalk as if she wasn't sure of her destination.

The man who'd been sitting at her table slid up beside her and cupped her elbow. When she tried to escape his grip, he held on tighter and pulled a fob out of his pocket, which he used to unlock a car further up the sidewalk.

Ryan took it as his cue to move, and eased up on the woman's other side.

Alarm spread over her face when their eyes met. Hers were out of focus and her pupils dilated. The traffic and the persons passing them on the sidewalk served to make her more confused.

"Do you know this man?" Ryan asked.

"N-no—"

"She's coming with me," the man with thick brows and a husky voice growled. "My car is over here."

"Think again." Ryan glanced at the woman, whose weight now rested on him. She seemed disoriented, which was evidence of what he thought the men had been trying to achieve.

A frown darkened the man's face. "But—"

"You have a problem?" Dro asked from behind him, raising his voice above the music coming from the club.

"This man needs to mind his own business. The woman is my friend. We were going—"

"What is her name?" Ryan challenged.

He shuffled his feet and huffed, "Uh, her name is Theresa."

"What's your name?" Ryan asked gently, to avoid startling the woman in his arms.

"Carol," she whispered. "I think I'm going to be sick."

"Wrong answer. He isn't legit," Ryan said to Dro, leading Carol to the nearest receptacle. He held back her braids as she released the contents of her stomach into the massive sidewalk flowerpot. Then he offered his handkerchief, which she accepted.

"Hey!" the man called. "She's coming with me."

"Not today, José." Dro spun to face Bashir and the other two men emerging from the bar. "Do not come any closer if you know what's good for you."

One man snarled, "You cannot stop us from taking her."

"Really?"

As the two accomplices advanced on Dro, Ryan tensed but was in no position to assist. From what Shaz told him, Dro was an expert at hand-to-hand combat, but he wasn't sure about Bashir. Ryan beckoned to him.

Bashir was at his side immediately.

"Take care of her," he said, maneuvering so that Carol's weight now rested on Bashir.

"Thank you," she whispered.

Ryan took two hurried steps, but needn't have bothered. The two men lay unconscious on the sidewalk, and Dro was in the middle of delivering a roundhouse kick to the third.

A crowd spilled through the front door of the club. Among them was Jahani Bahar, the bartender. When their eyes met, he glared at Dro and spun away with a phone pressed to his ear.

Ryan plunged into the crowd after him.

"Where are you going?" Dro yelled.

"After that bartender. Don't let Carol out of your sight."

Chapter 9

The air thickened as the container creaked open. Hamid stepped inside, escorting Naima by the arm. The tense atmosphere dissipated for the moment. Then despair hung in the air when Abdul appeared and forced a young Black girl ahead of him. She cradled her arm against her side while tears flooded her cheeks.

Aziza propped herself on one elbow as Naima approached.

Blood trickled from the corner of her mouth. One of her eyes was swollen shut. Her face was wet with perspiration and tears. When she sat on the cot, Hamid secured her wrist and pointed to the empty bed next to Aziza. None of the other women moved, as if afraid they would be abused if they even shifted.

Hamid threw Naima an apologetic glance before leaving her side. He moved to the new girl, who didn't appear to be more than sixteen. She wore Bantu knots in her hair and clutched the top of her torn house dress with one hand. Her tears hadn't stopped, and she curled into a ball on her side. She pleaded with Hamid in words Aziza didn't understand, but it didn't help her case.

With his job of tethering her done, Hamid left.

Aziza's gaze shot to where Abdul stood. Fury simmered behind his eyes. As Hamid went past him, Abdul's face twisted and he shot Naima a killing look, then limped toward the doorway.

A smirk pulled at Aziza's lips until her focus turned to her friend, who lay trembling as her tears soaked the dingy sheet. Shaking with anger, Aziza asked, "Did Abdul hurt you?"

Naima sniffed and shook her head. In her lilting accent, she explained, "He tried to rape me, but I kicked him in the crotch."

Leaning toward her, Aziza said, "I could tell you put a hurting on him. That'll teach him."

With a fist tucked under her head, Naima sobbed. When her tears subsided, she spoke in a monotone. "If I had known this would happen to me, I never would have left Senegal."

A pang of sorrow hit Aziza, and she lay on her back. She didn't have time to sink any lower because the door opened again. This time, they had a visitor—a short man, shrouded by a *kaffiyeh* that only left his gleaming eyes visible. They ran greedily over the females, then rested on the youngest. With an imperious gesture, his finger flicked toward four children of African descent. None of them was over twelve years old. He hesitated over the East Indian girl, who shrieked uncontrollably the moment his gaze fell on her.

Unable to bear the hopelessness in the eyes of the girls and their anguished cries, Aziza closed her eyes, but that didn't stop bitter tears from escaping. When the container slammed shut and their screams faded, Aziza drew a harsh breath and said a prayer to keep herself from falling deeper into a place from which she wouldn't be able to rise.

The other women groaned, and some wept openly. Nothing had prepared any of them for this kind of horror.

Her father's voice washed over her, and she pictured him roughhousing with Drake when he was thirteen. Her brother was skinny and reserved, which made him a target for bullies. When he revealed what was happening to him at school, their father taught him how to fight back.

George Hampton was a physical education teacher and had cemented it into their heads that their greatest strength was not physical, but mental. In life, Aziza had proven his words to be true. All she achieved came through hard work and using the brain and smarts God gave her. However freedom came, it would be hers.

She opened her eyes and met those of the little Indian girl. Aziza dredged up a weak smile.

After a moment of staring at her with a solemn expression, the child returned her gesture.

"What is your name?" Aziza asked, propping herself on one elbow.

The girl mirrored her position. "Sunita."

"Don't worry. We will be all right."

Sunita chewed her lip as if digesting her words, then she nodded and dragged her sleeve across her face to dry her tears.

Aziza felt awful about what amounted to lying. She had no guarantee any of them would survive this horror. All she had was faith in God. She had to bring her trust in Ryan to that level and hope he'd somehow know she needed him more than she had at any other time.

Ever since she arrived in Durabia, she'd been careful, but somehow she fell into the same trap as all these other women. From the headache, nausea, and heaviness in her limbs when she first arrived in this makeshift prison, she understood that someone spiked her drink.

Betrayal wouldn't fully express how she'd feel if she found out someone she worked with did the deed. If it wasn't one of them, it had to be the bartender or one of the servers. She didn't need to ask why. Money was the driving force behind kidnapping. That's if they didn't plan to stuff them full of contraband and force them to be drug mules.

She changed the direction of her thoughts. Negative thinking would not help. Now, it was urgent to get out of this hell-hole before her turn came for them to sell her. Whatever it took, she had to do something before the day ended. Tomorrow wasn't promised in this location if they had any buyers coming through today.

Ryan's face floated before her eyes and she blinked, surprised to find her cheeks wet again. She longed to bask in the glow of his good-natured grin and suggestive comments about what he'd do to her when next they were together. He was the total opposite of the man she'd been with before him. Where Ryan was free with his affection, Eric had been close-mouthed and stingy with compliments. She didn't need him to bolster her self-esteem, but encouragement from her partner was something she expected.

Plus, he was a serial cheater. By the time their relationship ended, Aziza wondered what she'd seen in him. When she dumped him, his parting remark was that she'd never been pretty enough or smart enough for him. His malice didn't affect her because she understood that somewhere inside, he was broken. Not that he'd ever admit it.

The continued sobbing from the teenager on her other side interrupted Aziza's mental flow. The scent of urine hung around her and assaulted her nose. Aziza raised her head. "Do you speak English?"

With her expressive doe eyes shimmering, she nodded.

"What's your name and where are you from?"

"It is Ahaba Ysrael. I am from Liberia." She pulled in a deep breath and held out her hand. "My employer did this. When I couldn't take care of the baby or clean the house, she … "

Ahaba dissolved in tears, while Aziza shivered involuntarily and hid her shock at the gaping patch of pink flesh on the girl's arm. The shape of the wound looked as if someone had held a hot iron to her arm.

"Oh my God," Naima gasped. "That's just wicked. Why would anyone … "

Aziza shushed her, then whispered. "Now is not the time. What we need to do is get the keys from Hamid when he comes to give us dinner."

Alarm filled Naima's eyes. "I don't want to think about what Abdul will do if we fail."

Leaning toward her, Aziza said, "I can't think about us not succeeding. That isn't an option." She pointed to the other women. "We all agreed that we're going to do this. Don't back out on me now."

A verbal exchange on the other side of the container interrupted their hushed conversation. Both of them cocked their heads, but from Naima's mystified expression, Aziza knew she didn't understand what was being said. She identified Abdul and Hamid's voices, but the other two men with them were strangers. Or so she thought.

When Ahaba released a small shriek, then clapped a hand to her mouth, Aziza turned concerned eyes on her. "What is it?"

Ahaba kept a hand over her lips, but pointed in the direction where the chatter continued. Perspiration poured from her forehead, and her tears would not stop. As she drew labored breaths, Aziza's shoulders sank and anxiety filled her belly. "What are they saying?"

Ahaba's jaw wobbled as she said, "They are talking about which one of us they will gut for our organs."

Chapter 10

"You still with me, Ryan?" Shaz prompted from the screen.

"It's a lot to absorb if you haven't ever seen anything like this before," Dro said from the corner of Ryan's room that overlooked the pool.

"Yeah, it's enough to turn the strongest stomach." Ryan pulled in a deep breath to continue, "How the hell can people do this to other human beings?"

They gained access to the pictures of the two women on his screen through Daron Kincaid, who arrived on schedule, a day after Dro. The dark-haired security expert had come straight to Ryan's room for a mini-conference.

"For the money," Dro said over his shoulder, facing the plate glass.

"And remember … " Shaz tipped his head toward the screen. "There are folks out there who think Black people are less than human. It's easy when you look at these women as dispensable."

Ryan nodded. "I get it. If that policeman viewed George Floyd as his equal and therefore worthy of respect, he'd never have put a knee to his neck."

"That's right, and it took a worldwide protest to make that point," Shaz said. "Let's get the bastards who thought it was okay to kill these women for their organs and dump them like so much garbage."

"Whoever did the job is an expert surgeon, based on these images." Ryan rubbed his temples and pulled his mind away from the dark path it had taken. This would not be Aziza's fate.

Daron sat next to Ryan at an oval meeting table positioned to one side of the cream-and-gold suite. The Sheikh and Sheikha offered them accommodations, but they thought it best to stay where Aziza had spent most of her time. Daron planned to move around the country, following clues as necessary, so he agreed to stay at Khalil's palace. "So, aside from the game they're running at Encounters, we have no leads. Is that correct?" he asked.

Pacing the room, Dro weighed in. "That place is a hub for some nasty activity."

"That's right, and I believe we're on to something," Ryan said, including Shaz in his comment. "The authorities do not believe this is even worth their attention. Our visit did not change their attitude. Only the hint of scandal and the threat of reporting to the Sheikh meant anything to them. The attempted kidnapping charge we tried to bring did not stick. That bartender and the other two were released within an hour of being picked up by the police."

"Where's the woman, Carol?" Shaz asked.

"We took her to Jai's medical facility. They did some tests and found drugs in her system. Jai arranged for her to go home when she felt better. Hopefully, she's learned from this experience."

"So, d'you have a plan?" Shaz asked.

"I sure do," Ryan said, glancing between Daron and Dro. "Between these two, they have expertise in crisis management, security, and gadgetry. I know those punks at Encounters are up to no good." He put a hand to his chest. "Based on what I saw, I know it in here. We should put a tail on them and see where it leads. Trafficking and organ harvesting are big business. They're not about to give it up because we intercepted them last night."

"So, about that plan … " Dro laid a hand on Ryan's shoulder.

With a chuckle, Ryan said, "I'm getting to it, don't get in a rush."

"If I hear you clearly," Dro said, "This is where we get involved. We lay some bait and see if they bite."

"Exactly." Ryan nodded. "I like your style."

"We'll need manpower to have them followed," Daron said. "Nicco and Angela came over with me, so we have that angle covered."

He took a moment to explain to Ryan that Nicco had formed part of his mentor's protective detail after an assassination attempt and had been instrumental in rescuing the Sheikha from her kidnappers. Nicco had also been assigned to protect Calvin Atwood, a brilliant scientist in high demand for his inventions. By the sound of it, Daron had brought in two formidable security experts.

"Can you plant a bug on that bartender?" As Dro paced, he shoved one hand through his dark hair. "What's his name again?"

"Jahani Bahar," Ryan supplied, remembering how the guy gave him the slip when he followed him back inside the club.

"Yes, we can organize that," Daron said. "Sheikh Kamran's all for putting in manpower and whatever else we need to rid Durabia of the corruption that ran rampant under his father's rule."

Ryan cocked one brow and shifted so he was face to face with Daron. "And how will that bug be planted?"

Dro grinned. "We shouldn't worry about that because we can count on Daron for a workable plan."

"Let's hear it," Shaz said, reaching for a gizzada and crunching the sugary coconut-and-flour concoction between his teeth.

"We need to get to the heart of this operation, to smash it in one blow." Daron stopped spinning his hat and hung it on one knee. "Spying on the bartender will give us a leg up the ladder, so we can find out who is the brain behind this operation."

"Hang on a minute." Shaz dusted crumbs from his hands, frowning. "Let's go back to that bug. How are we going to get it planted?"

"That's what I want to know, too." Ryan's gaze shifted to Daron. "And where will it go, plus how will it happen, 'cause I don't see it."

Dro's smile was lopsided. "That's because you don't quite know how ingenious our tech man can be."

Chuckling, Daron said, "Any second now I'll be wondering what you're after and why you're laying it on so thick."

"Can't a King brag about his brother's skills without you getting suspicious?" Dro said with a comedic lift of his eyebrows.

They all laughed, then Daron set his hat on the low table behind him. He waggled one finger between Dro and Ryan. "You two can't be back in the club any time soon after yesterday's shenanigans. I'll get hold of the bar man's work schedule for today."

"I know better than to ask how you're gonna get that information, so go on." Shaz raised one hand for Daron to continue.

"I'll use Angela as a distraction and get the listening device stuck to his badge or vest. That will give us a bead on who he's talking to and possibly the identity of the other players in this business."

"You're *that* sure of her powers of seduction?" Ryan asked.

"Trust me. She's all that. Angela is relatively new to my team, but has a wide array of skills which you all don't need to know about right now."

"Sound like she's dangerous to tangle with, too," Dro added.

The door handle sank, and all three men looked toward the doorway.

"You expecting anyone?" Dro asked, moving one hand to the back of his waist.

Ryan shook his head and slid the desk drawer open. His Beretta rested inside.

The light in the lock flashed green, then the door opened. A stocky man, a local, looked both ways down the corridor before he walked into the room. His eyes widened as he slid the keycard into his pocket. "I didn't know anyone was here."

He forced a smile, then motioned to the supply cart behind him. "Sorry to interrupt. I am here to take care of the room."

"Thank you, but we're busy." Ryan said.

The houseman's gaze swept across the laptop screen, then he bowed touching a hand to his white tunic with the hotel's logo on the chest. "I will return when it's convenient."

"There's no need," Ryan said, sliding the drawer shut.

"Are you sure, sir?" The houseman's eyes strayed back to the screen, where Shaz watched him. "It's hotel policy—"

"He said it's fine," Dro got to his feet.

The man backed away. "I just wanted to be sure—"

Ryan spoke under his breath, "Just go already."

When the door closed, Daron asked, "Am I the only one who thinks there's something off about him?"

"He was too interested in what we had going on," Shaz said, reaching for a glass of water. "Best keep your eyes open, little cousin."

Ryan rolled his eyes. They barely had two years between them. A smile bloomed on his face, along with a spark of mischief. "Anything you say, Shastra."

He shot Ryan a glare. "Good thing you're out of my reach, otherwise you'd feel the force of my fist."

Ryan slapped his knee and chuckled. "Right."

The two of them were equally matched on a physical level, as Shaz knew, but their light-hearted teasing was a constant in their relationship.

Shaz's smile disappeared. "I'm serious about your security. You're far away from home, and I don't want any of you in more danger than necessary."

"I hear you," Ryan said, to reassure his cousin. "But I doubt these men need you worrying about them."

"Whatever. Just remember that at the end of the day, they're my brothers. They hurt. I hurt."

"That, I also get loud and clear."

Dro stalked toward the door without a word.

"Hey, where are you going?" Ryan asked.

"To see if this guy is legit," Dro said over his shoulder.

"Need company?" Daron asked.

"No. I don't want him to get suspicious. I'll be back in a few."

"Be careful," the men all said at the same time, including Shaz.

When the door closed, Ryan turned his gaze on Daron. "I know I'm probably annoying the crap out of you, but are you sure we can get this bug in place tonight?"

He stood to stretch his legs, and with one hand massaging the back of his head, he added, "I have a lot riding on this and will do anything to get Aziza back. If we don't find my woman, I don't know what I'll do. But one thing is sure, somebody will have to pay if she doesn't return safe and sound."

Chapter 11

Aziza wound her head in a circle and drew her shoulders back. The girls taken earlier weighed on her mind, and her thoughts had been running in different directions as she mapped out a way to freedom. She rubbed her forehead and released another prayer.

Father, we need your help. These girls, these women, we need you. Give us the strength to defeat our enemies and give me the courage to lead the way. And Father, watch over Ryan, wherever he may be.

By now, surely her mother had raised an alarm. The first thing she probably did was contact Shaz Bostwick, because he'd know how to reach Ryan, plus he and his wife headed a foundation that helped women with custody and immigration challenges. She clung to the hope that Shaz would have contacted Ryan and urged him to do something to help. If, between them, they did nothing she wouldn't forgive them. Ahaba's words still chilled her. Of all the things she'd imagined in life, none of it included being used as a means of shipping contraband for greedy criminals.

If they don't come in time, I might wake up on the other side, freshly gutted and—

"Say a prayer for me."

Naima's whispered words shook Aziza from her thoughts. She searched the other woman's eyes. "Of course. Are you sure you want to do this?"

Her swollen eye chided Aziza as she said, "Do I have a choice? If we want our freedom … "

The container opened, and an oppressive cloud descended to suck away the life-giving air.

"Remember to keep him busy long enough to—"

"I get it," Naima said.

"Here." Aziza handed her the hook she'd removed from the shower curtain.

Naima twisted it into her braids and secured them. Then, she squared her shoulders as Hamid walked toward them.

The plan they came up with was to get Abdul to believe Naima had reconsidered her position and would have sex with him in exchange for whatever favor he gave. The way his beady eyes roamed Naima's body gave them hope he would say yes, and they were right. Aziza hoped he wouldn't take revenge when he was alone with Naima, for that disarming kick to his genitals.

Aziza steadied her breath and nodded at Naima. "Be careful," she whispered.

Eyes closed, Naima squared her shoulders.

Hamid released her from the handcuff and led her to where Abdul stood waiting. When he grabbed Naima by the upper arm and shunted her out of the container, Aziza called Hamid's name.

He looked over his shoulder at the open container door, shifted the rifle he carried on his shoulder, then faced her.

"I need to use the bathroom."

Hamid slammed the door shut, latched it, and walked toward her bed.

"It's urgent," she said, sitting up and pulling her thighs together.

He cast another glance at the door, then beckoned to her.

She had to move fast, and his sluggish pace wasn't helping.

As soon as he unlocked the shackle, she shot to her feet and waited at the door that led to the bathroom. He opened it with a key from the bunch, and she rushed past him on her bare feet. She urinated, despite the limited liquid in her system, knowing the sound would carry to

Hamid through the half-open door. As her thoughts raced, Aziza flushed the toilet.

Earlier, she pictured frame-by-frame how she had spent her summers of the past with her brother and Ryan. They had taught her some kickboxing and karate moves they learned at the rec center. Both boys insisted that she learn how to take care of herself. Shame she hadn't thought to use those skills to help herself before this minute. Her mother's face flashed before her, but Aziza blinked to clear her eyes and focused on the present moment. She washed her hands and opened the flimsy wooden panel with her elbow.

Hamid watched her, but not with the care of the first couple of days. When she was directly in front of him, she rammed her elbow into his solar plexus. He gasped, and the rifle slid off his shoulder. She swung her body into the next blow and hit him in the same spot. This time his eyes bulged.

"Sorry," she whispered as he crumpled against the wall.

But that didn't stop her from walloping him with a fist to his jaw.

She grabbed the keys from his hand, along with the rifle. As she stood, he wrapped a hand around her ankle. Without blinking, she shook him off and delivered a swift kick to his ribs. Then she cracked him on the side of the head with the butt of the rifle. He grunted and slumped on his side.

She shut down her thoughts. Her options were him or her, and she'd choose freedom over being sliced open like a fish any day.

Aziza rushed out of the narrow space, slammed the door behind her, and with shaking hands searched for the key he'd used on their way in. She locked him inside, then spun from the door and took the few steps to Ahaba, who held up her uninjured hand.

After freeing her, Aziza went to each bed and unlocked the handcuff. As she did, the women's voice rose in a wave of excitement.

"Keep it down," she commanded.

When they discussed their escape days earlier, none of them knew what lay beyond the confines of their prison, but most of them were willing to take their chances. Now that she thought about it, they were hiding them in a remote location. The only time she remembered hearing any engines was when Abdul and Hamid had buyers.

She said a prayer that Naima would find a way to buy time other than giving Abdul access to her body. The first time Naima proposed that she distract Abdul, Aziza had refused. A man like that didn't forget anything, and Naima's earlier abuse of his manly parts wouldn't be forgiven. But Naima had already proven she could handle her business, so Aziza gave in and agreed to manage Hamid. The thought of him brought a pang of guilt, but she brushed it away. If she wanted to return home, she had to concentrate on what lay ahead of her.

She was unlocking the last handcuff when Hamid yelled and banged on the door. If she'd known he would wake so soon, she'd have hit him harder.

One of the women, a Durabian native, worked the heavy bolt, which creaked as if it never had the benefit of a drop of oil. She swung the metal door inward wearing a beatific smile, which slid away in a second.

Naima landed in a heap in front of them as Abdul shouted a rapid-fire string of words. One side of his face carried four diagonal lines that seeped blood. The women helped Naima to her feet and formed a protective shield around her.

"Get back," he said, yanking out a pistol from under his tunic. "Or all of you will die."

"Wanna bet?" Aziza picked up the rifle and walked into his line of sight, aiming at his belly. "Since we are valuable goods, your boss would kill *you* if we died."

Fear flashed in his eyes, but his hand was steady as he pointed the gun at her. "Where is Hamid?"

She shifted the gun. "I'd say that's unimportant, given the position you're in."

"I am giving you until the count of three," Abdul said, in heavily accented English. "One. Two."

A whirlwind rushed past Aziza and toppled Abdul.

The gun fell from his hand as Naima sprawled in the sand between his legs.

"Aaaahhhhh." He shrieked and writhed on the ground while Naima gripped a handful of his genitals.

In the distance beyond a low fence, two men approached, wearing tunics like Abdul and Hamid. They also carried semi-automatic weapons.

Grabbing Naima's shoulder, Aziza spoke into her ear. "Let go, or they will catch us."

Then throwing a panicked look towards the men, who advanced on them, Aziza yelled, "Naima, let him go now!"

Naima released Abdul and stumbled to her feet with anger blazing in her eyes.

"Get him inside," Aziza yelled, as Abdul groaned and curled on his side.

One woman picked up the gun and the others grabbed him by both hands and hauled him onto the cement deck and then over the threshold of the container.

"And be sure to cuff him," she added, and threw a glance behind her.

Aziza backed toward their prison, only to be shoved in the back by Ahaba, who trampled Abdul and ran onto the sand. "I can't go back," she cried.

Her eyes were wild with fear, but Aziza didn't have time to mollycoddle her. "If you want to be shot, you can leave. Otherwise, get back inside."

She didn't move, but her glossy eyes gave away her confusion.

The men drew closer, their weapons drawn.

Aziza didn't dare to lower the rifle, although her arms trembled from the adrenaline pumping through her veins and the strain of keeping the AK-47 upright. Over her shoulder, she yelled. "They have weapons." To Ahaba, she said, "I'm not leaving you out here. Get your ass back inside."

After another look at the men, Ahaba ran into the container.

Aziza drew a calming breath, repositioned the rifle now numbing her arms, and focused on the men in front of her.

Chapter 12

"Remember, you are *not* taking part in this." Daron said from the front of the Limousine, then let his gaze swing between Dro and Ryan.

"We get it." Dro held up both hands in surrender. "We'll sit this one out, as requested."

Daron chuckled, smoothing his silk shirt. "You have it all wrong. Consider my recommendation an order. The two of you will be safer here."

"Where no one will recognize us." Ryan groused, then nodded. "We get it."

Bashir cracked a smile, but didn't speak.

"You're not coming either," Daron said to him, "Just in case you thought otherwise."

Bashir's smile faded.

"Angela and Nicco, time to roll."

They stepped onto the sidewalk and immediately, the people waiting to get into Encounters turned to stare. Ryan admitted they made an impressive sight—one curvaceous, olive-skinned woman, a Nordic giant, and a dark-haired man, who oozed assurance.

Bashir, who assumed the role of chauffeur, drove them to the parking garage down the street where Dro opened his laptop and they settled in to follow their movements inside the club. While Daron and his team were on location, they would scan the surroundings from the cameras worn by all three. The club had a good number of people moving around both levels. Seemed that no matter the day of the week, Encounters was in vogue.

He had to give Angela her due when she walked up to the counter, waited a few seconds, then got the bartender's attention.

Jahani was on duty this evening.

As Angela spoke to him, his eyes followed her curves with each move she made, and his attention did not stray when she walked away carrying a cocktail glass.

She set herself up at a table twenty feet away from Daron and Nicco.

From Daron's camera, they had a view of the bar, and Nicco's recorder covered another angle that included the front entrance.

"Nicco if you move your seat a little, we can get a better look at the tables with the single ladies," Dro said.

"No problem." Nicco's voice came through crisp and clear via the mic while he adjusted his chair.

Angela rose from her seat and made a beeline for the bar. She placed her glass on the counter and signaled to Jahani. His gaze settled on her cleavage, where the mini camera was disguised as a rhinestone. Looking into his eyes startled Ryan, who felt helpless because they were sitting around waiting for information to drop.

If he had his way, they'd drag that slimy bartender over the counter and beat the crap out of him until he spilled what they wanted to know. But like his mother told him through the years, 'patient man ride donkey.' The phrase almost made him chuckle, being one of his grandmother's favorites, too. She'd moved to Evanston from Jamaica many years ago, but you couldn't tell because she never lost her accent from home or her patience with the youngest member of the Bostwick family. He had learned a lot from her including when to call on The Man Upstairs.

Ryan shut off his memories and leaned in when Angela slid the glass across the counter and motioned for the bartender to come nearer. The man's close-set eyes seemed to bore into Ryan's. Then his gaze shifted upward when Angela edged toward him.

"I'd like a top-up," she said.

"That will not be a problem." He smiled, then winked. "Give me a minute."

He dealt with another customer while the other bar staff hustled back and forth behind the counter, serving drinks. Jahani returned with her order and set it on the counter.

Angela slid the cherry into her mouth while Jahani watched, then handed him the toothpick. She beckoned to him again, and when he leaned forward, she laid a hand on his chest and whispered, "Thanks for taking care of me."

The bartender's skin flushed darker and with desire evident in his eyes, he said, "You are welcome. Maybe we can have a drink together later this evening."

"Yes, Jahani." She tapped his nametag and continued in a throaty voice. "We should."

Ryan had to admit she was smooth. As closely as he was watching, he barely caught the moment when she attached the mic to Jahani.

"How small is that bug?" Ryan squinted at the screen as if it would give up its secrets.

Dro chuckled. "So small that if he picks up on it, the chip will resemble a clump of dust particles, clinging to a sliver of plastic."

"Sounds slick."

"State-of-the-art and all that."

Angela sauntered back to her seat, then sipped from her glass as she glanced around the room, which pulsated with the sounds of Koffee's Rapture.

Ryan wanted to see some action now, but knew instinctively that any underhanded business would happen later in the evening. Eyes closed, he let out his breath on a long exhale.

"It's a little early for you to be exhausted," Dro teased, looking sideways at him.

"Nah, nothing like that. I was just thinking."

Dro nodded, his attention focused on the screen. "I know how it is when your other half is in danger and you don't have a clue how or why things happen the way they do."

"You hit the nail on the head."

"It happened to me with Lola. I nearly went mad when some criminal kidnapped her. Couldn't eat, sleep, or think about anything other than getting her back, so I understand. Khalil had my brother Kings knock me out so they would handle the business. They didn't want me to increase Chicago's body count." His lips quirked, then he added. "I won't tell you not to worry, but—"

"Trust me," Ryan said, shaking his head, "I'm not about that life. Worry solves nothing, but I feel you on putting some heat on somebody's ass."

"Good." Dro cracked a smile. "I want to reassure you, we'll be about this business as if she was one of our own—and she is. We'll get her back, alive and in one piece."

Despite the reassurance, Ryan sighed again. His energy was off and as long as he didn't fix that, he'd be no use to Dro. "D'you mind if I stretch my legs for a minute?"

Eyes fixed on the laptop, Dro waved him away. "Do what you have to do."

Ryan pushed the door open and walked to the railing a few feet away, to stare at the river. The city lights glinting on the surface distracted him from what he came to do. The wash of the water against the rocks below was hypnotic and as the wind ruffled his black shirt, he pulled in his breath and let it out. After listening to his breathing for a minute, Ryan poured his heart into a prayer, which included a healing request for Drake and comfort for the rest of the family. He shouldn't have left his room without praying, but as Mama would say, better to do it later than not at all.

Then he made declarations, claiming Aziza's safety and her quick return to him, which cleared his head and lightened his spirit.

"Thank you, Father," he whispered. "I believe and I *will* receive."

With renewed energy, he crossed the outdoor tiles between him and the Limo.

Bashir gave him a cursory glance as he approached the car with a purposeful stride.

He slid into the seat next to Dro and shut the door. "Anything yet?"

"You see that guy, there?" He pointed to someone sitting at a table across from the bar. "He and Jahani are exchanging signals. I think they're after that woman there."

The bi-racial East Indian female, who wore a red dress with a matching scarf, sat by herself sipping a drink.

"Are you seeing a pattern here?" Ryan asked.

"Yep, but it leaves the question of why they took Aziza when she was here with a group."

"Forgive my choice of words, but if you can separate your target from the herd, it makes the job easier."

"True that," Dro said.

Ryan sat forward. "Your bartender looks like he's about to take a break or something."

A man dressed in black nodded to Jahani, who tipped his head toward the back of the club. Five minutes later, Jahani said something to another bartender and walked through a door behind the bar.

When his voice hit them a moment later, the clarity was impressive. "We have one potential female, but I'd like to have her first."

Angela interrupted, translating their words from Arabic.

"We missed out last time because of those interfering foreigners." The man's harsh voice climbed as he uttered what Ryan assumed was a curse word. "Did you put something in her drink?"

"You expect me to do that and be out here talking with you?" Jahani asked. "It is early. We have time."

In an emphatic tone, his companion said, "We cannot afford to make any mistakes this time."

"I agree." Jahani chuckled. "I might have a little action later tonight. I wouldn't want anything to get in the way."

"As long as Fahid and the boss are happy, we—"

"No names," Jahani hissed. "How many times do I have to tell you?"

"Sorry. I won't forget again."

"I should hope not."

The music from the club intruded on the conversation as if they stepped back into the building. Then Jahani said, "I will give the woman in red the treatment in the next drink. Don't mess this up."

Chapter 13

"You will never escape." Abdul scowled, as if he thought it would intimidate her.

She turned on her bare heels. "If you don't shut up … "

"What will you do?" he taunted from where he lay propped on one elbow.

Aziza let her gaze stray to his crotch. "You don't want to know."

When he winced and drew his legs together, she smirked.

A force hit the door with the impact of a battering ram.

"What di hell is dat?" Kelsie asked in a pronounced Patois. The tall woman with braids and dark skin had proven herself proactive in the last half-hour. She organized the women in teams to pile the cots against the entrance. Then, she set about calming the young girls who fell apart as the threats from the men outside intensified. Her accent had the same nuances as that of her parents and her grandmother, so Aziza thought she was from Jamaica. That, she would investigate later, if she had the time and opportunity.

"Sounds like reinforcement," Aziza said, glancing at the gun she'd leaned in the corner. "But not for us."

Kelsie lifted the handgun they took from Abdul. "Don't worry. I know how to use this. I'll help you hold them off."

Worry gnawed at Aziza's stomach, but she maintained an air of confidence. No one else knew her secret. She'd watched Drake do internet searches that would have put fear into their mother, if she knew what he was doing online. Often enough, Aziza sat at his elbow and watched live videos of people handling guns and rifles. She wasn't a marksman by any stretch of the imagination. Heck, she hadn't ever touched a weapon before today, but she had a good idea of how to handle herself if it came to the test. God help anyone within range if she had to engage the AK-47.

Beckoning toward the bathroom, Aziza handed her the key. To all of them, she said, "Search this place and see what you can find to defend yourselves. Doesn't matter how large or small. Some of you go with Kelsie. Make sure you get all the shower hooks, plus whatever else you can find."

When they didn't move immediately, she shooed them. "Go on. We can't be at their mercy. We have to protect ourselves and the kids."

The men continued to assault the door. From what she gathered, two other men had joined those who chased them down. She glanced at the gun, reassuring herself it was within easy reach.

"Who are they?" she asked, facing Abdul.

He stared at her as if he'd lost the ability to speak.

"Are they your business partners?"

Satisfaction gleamed in his eyes, but he didn't answer.

The hum of the air-conditioning stopped, and the women stared at each other. Someone had switched off the cooling system. The four narrow windows at the top of the container were sealed with glass, which limited the air flowing inside. The unrelenting heat promised to creep on them within minutes, making them miserable. Thank God they were at the back end of the day, but they needed a miracle—the sooner the better. Their only advantage was that the night offered cooler temperatures.

At the far end of the room, Hamid sat on a cot with his head lowered. He, too, was chained to the metal frame. His eyes met Aziza's, but she looked away. She didn't have time to regret how she treated him, never mind the fact that the way he made his living was outside of the law.

"If you do not open this door now, we will shoot."

"Well, so will I," Aziza yelled, then immediately realized her mistake. She waved madly at the women, motioning for them to get down on the floor. Then she followed her instinct, flipped the lights off, and squatted. If these men kept up a sustained attack, they would shred the metal and kill them all.

A hail of bullets descended. The women panicked and scrambled to the back of the container, amid blood-curdling screams. When they huddled against each other on the floor, Aziza scuttled toward them on her hands and knees. She put a finger to her lips, then spoke in a stage whisper, following her own instructions as she gave them. "Keep it down and get on your bellies."

To the echo of sniffles and whimpers, they spread out. The stench of fear hung heavy around them, then a ripple of whispers spread as the women prayed. Aziza did her fair share as she lay listening to the men circling outside. *Like hyenas coming in to devour their prize.*

One of them shouted what sounded like a question.

Ahaba's head popped up. Rushing her words out, she said, "He is asking where we are."

In the light slanting in from outside, Aziza gave Hamid a look meant to keep him quiet, then crouched and ran back to Abdul, who shouted an answer. She socked him in the gut, which stopped him in the middle of informing.

"Shut the hell up."

With his hands protecting his belly, he continued to talk but winced as he shifted onto his side away from her.

Aziza ripped the turban off his head and lowered it to his mouth. Though he fought her, she yanked it into a knot, then tied the end of it again. His greasy black hair was rancid, but she ignored the offensive smell as she straddled him.

He tried heaving her off, but she had been smart enough to ensure they secured both of his hands, which left him with a limited range of motion.

With her weight, she pressed him to the bed and delivered two blows to the side of his head. Pain radiated up through her wrist into her arm. If she kept this up, her fist would be of little use for anything after today.

With hate-filled eyes, Abdul breathed hard into the fabric of his turban. She could well imagine how outraged he was at having a woman handle him this way, and a Black one at that. At the thought of the unknown victims he'd sold into slavery, Aziza clocked him again.

"Listen to me, you useless piece of shit, you'll get all of us killed. And if they don't murder us, I'll shoot you myself when this is over."

Abdul wriggled and mumbled while she still sat on him. He didn't plan to go down without a fight. He was a worthy opponent, who had smelled blood. Aziza's energy had run out. She hated the disgusting slop they fed them and only ate enough to stay alive. Right now she was running on adrenaline and desperation. Her dilemma ended when Naima appeared over her shoulder and smacked Abdul hard enough to put him out.

"Thank you," Aziza whispered.

Another round of gunfire had the two of them diving off the bed. The younger girls bit their fists to hold in their screams. Naima met Aziza's eyes as tears welled in hers. She brushed them away with one hand, then they both crab-walked to the group. Naima settled back in position next to Ahaba and slipped an arm around her shoulder. The teenager burrowed her face against Naima's neck.

"We are going to make it," Aziza whispered to Naima, who rested her sweating forehead against the back of her hand. She continued whispering that mantra as the darkness deepened around them.

Although believing they would get out of this situation was hard, Aziza had no choice. She would hang on to her faith and continue to believe God wouldn't cut her time with Ryan short before she could enjoy him properly. She had to trust that no matter how impossible the odds seemed, he would find her.

The men fired again.

Hamid's scream turned her blood to ice.

Chapter 14

Even with a black eye, the bartender stayed defiant.

Daron and his team had foiled the attempt to drug and kidnap the woman from Encounters earlier in the evening.

Somewhat.

Now, they were at a standoff.

Jahani refused to communicate with them in English, although they knew he spoke the language. Most people in the service industry did. The chains on his hands and feet rattled as he shifted and re-settled on the chair.

Daron and Nicco had waited for Jahani and his partner to make a move before swooping down on the slight man attempting to steer the dazed woman into a car. The modus operandi was the same as last time, but Jahani's partner in crime was different.

Angela and Nicco had followed the car and would report back as soon as they could convey his destination. Bashir was dispatched to update the Sheikh and Sheikha of the developments. His errand would keep him occupied elsewhere until they pinpointed the women's location. He'd opened his mouth to call bull shiggity, but at the last moment, he walked away to do the job without complaint. Bashir had done nothing to earn Ryan's suspicion, but he preferred their operation to have every chance at success. They were so close to finding out where they kept the kidnap victims.

Ryan stayed on tenterhooks, barely able to remain motionless. He wanted to bludgeon Jahani until he told them what they wanted to know, but Daron, Dro, and Vikkas wouldn't let him. So, here they were treating the bartender like royalty when he still didn't know if his woman was even in Durabia.

"Patience." Dro gripped his arm and led him to a far corner of the warehouse Sheikh Kamran had put at their disposal. Since his wife, Sheikha Ellena, had been kidnapped, he had a zero-tolerance policy for human trafficking. The fact that it had been his own family at the center of that plot made it all the more disheartening. But their underhanded maneuver also showed how deep the old ways and values were ingrained in those who had some semblance of power—especially when it came to women. When Daron requested the use of the warehouse to set up surveillance equipment, he didn't hesitate to say yes.

Dro slid both hands into his pockets and turned intense brown eyes on Ryan. "We *will* get him to talk and we're going to find her."

Waving a hand toward where Jahani sat, Ryan spoke through his teeth. "Every minute we spend treating him like he deserves any courtesy, it's more time for them to move her."

"Say what?" Wearing a slight smile, Dro added, "Nobody's trying to make things comfortable for this lowlife. The more information we get out of him, the better we'll be able to shut everything down when we strike."

When Ryan sighed, Dro said, "We can't get the data we need if we let you at him again. If we were anywhere else in the world, you would have an assault charge facing you. Thank God you have friends in high places."

Ryan still didn't speak, but threw a glare at Jahani.

"Everything in good time. Nicco and Angela are top-shelf pros. You can bet everything you have that they will get results. Let's finish up here." Dro met his eyes again. "*Without* you putting your fist in anyone's face. Capisce?"

"I get it," Ryan said in a grudging tone.

Dro squeezed his shoulder. "Let's get back to business."

Ryan pulled in a breath and shelved the fantasies he had of pulverizing the man he was sure had a hand in Aziza's disappearance.

At the sight of Ryan, a wary expression crept over Jahani's face, then resentment simmered in his eyes. His gaze slid to Dro, then back to Daron, who sat across from him. "Look, you can either help us *and* help yourself. Or … "

A hint of fear shrouded Jahani, and he lowered his head. Then, he spoke with his gaze fixed on his hands. "I cannot tell you what you wish to know."

"So, you prefer to spend the rest of your life behind bars for human trafficking rather—"

He sat up, almost smiling. "The fines for that are not very steep, so—"

Daron stared at him for a moment. "When the Sheikh has a personal stake in an investigation,"—He stabbed the surface of the metal desk between them—"things look a little different."

His words had an immediate effect.

Sweat dotted the bartender's forehead, and he couldn't sit still.

The silence took on an ominous quality.

Ryan almost believed the shadows at the edges of the room took on a life of their own, until Daron continued speaking.

"You need to decide what you will trade for the ability to keep your freedom."

Jahani sputtered while his attention darted to each man, who watched him, their faces impassive.

"Since you have all the time in the world," Vikkas said, motioning to Ryan. "We're about to pick up some supplies. Maybe by the time we return, Daron will have you back to your senses."

"What stuff are we picking up?" Ryan asked when he stood outside in the cool air with the other two men.

Vikkas beckoned to him with one finger and strode toward the car. "Let's just say, according to what Nicco thinks we'll come up against, we may need more firepower than anticipated."

"And you're saying to me ... " Ryan raised both brows and spoke to the man on his other side. " ... you left that sort of firepower unattended at the hotel?"

Dro grinned and tossed him the key to the Limo. "We're not saying any such thing. Let's put some speed on it, so we can get back here in a hurry."

Ryan took the wheel, glancing at Dro now and then in the rearview mirror. He was completely focused on the tablet in his hands, as if everything depended on what he was doing. Vikkas held his silence, frowning as if deep in thought.

Keeping his own counsel, Ryan drove back to the hotel and agreed to meet them in the lobby within ten minutes. The two sat in a corner of the lobby with their heads together while Ryan headed into the elevator.

The moment he stepped inside his room, Ryan's senses were on high alert. He couldn't put his finger on what was different, but knew someone had invaded his space. After scanning the entire suite, he put his unease down to the sixth sense he'd carried since birth until his gaze went to his laptop. The computer was open the way he normally left it, but the angle of the screen wasn't the same. Someone had been snooping. His mind went straight to the houseman who appeared earlier in the day. Dro had said little, except that the man would think twice about minding Ryan's business whenever he returned to take care of the room. If someone else was responsible, how did they get in and what were they seeking? If they were looking for digital information, they wouldn't have been able to get past Ryan's password and security measures.

On a hunch, he went to the safe and retrieved the wireless bug detector Daron had supplied. While he went through the suite sweeping every piece of furniture, someone rapped at the door.

Ryan stalked to the passage, wondering if the two Kings had come up to meet him. He depressed the handle, smiling. "I guess you two couldn't wait for—"

The man who faced him was Durabian. His thick mustache stirred a distant memory, but Ryan couldn't place him. The gleam in his eyes put Ryan on guard, along with the hand concealed behind his body. He crowded the door, but Ryan was prepared. He stepped back, planted his feet, and watched for the hand he couldn't see.

As the man rushed inside, Ryan swung the door, hitting him in the face. The force of his body colliding with the door nearly toppled Ryan, who released the handle. The stranger's hand whipped out from behind him in a jabbing motion.

Ryan grabbed his wrist, squeezed, then pulled him into a chokehold. With his other hand, he grabbed the taser and slammed it on the man's chest.

As he convulsed and his body went slack, Ryan's mental eyes came into sharp focus and he knew where he'd seen the man before this incident.

Ryan tased him a second time, then allowed him to fall to the carpet. As his eyes rolled back, Ryan kicked the door shut and pulled out his phone. He speed dialed Dro's number.

"I was about to call you."

"You'll be very interested in who's in my room." His gaze went to the man thrashing at his feet. "Get up here and make it quick."

Chapter 15

Ryan and Dro half walked, half carried the intruder to their car. He fought them as they dragged him into the service elevator under threat of another taste of the taser. Luck was on their side, and they were able to get him into the Limo under the cover of darkness, without calling attention to themselves. Vikkas helped them give the impression of a group of friends out for a jaunt, except for the large duffle he carried that belonged to Dro.

Now that the vehicle was at a standstill, their prisoner kept up a sustained hammering against the trunk. He was probably terrified in the clustered space, his mouth covered with electrical tape and both hands secured with plastic handcuffs.

Nicco's call to alert them that the bartender's accomplice was on the move, forced Ryan to drive with a leaden foot on the gas to get them to the warehouse before Daron's departure.

Dro got out of the vehicle and stood at the ready when Ryan opened the trunk.

The man inside was disheveled—clothes rumpled, hair falling into his eyes, and his skin drenched with sweat. His eyes popped wide as he tried talking through the tape. No doubt, he thought he was about to be murdered.

They ignored his protests while Dro informed Daron they had arrived.

As the door slid open, Daron said, "Good timing. We need to move. Be sure you all grab a helmet, just in case."

They shunted their prisoner inside, sat him in a chair at the opposite end of the building, and secured him to it with another pair of handcuffs. Then, they did as Daron instructed.

Jahani watched them, but didn't move or speak.

Their new prisoner continued making noises through the tape as they walked toward the door. They stopped and Ryan strode back to the man.

"You have something to say?" He ripped the tape away.

The man howled, then grimaced. A patch of hair was missing from his mustache. He spat words Ryan was sure were curses. The man's tirade didn't move him. He was more upset because they had nothing to show after chasing greedy, ruthless people.

"I am a member of the security forces. You will be in serious trouble for your actions."

"Maybe you should take your own advice." Ryan replaced the tape over his mouth. "While we're gone, think about the reason you came to my room to harm me."

The man's eyes flashed, and he lapsed into silence.

From the other side of the warehouse came the echo of the rattling chains on Jahani's hands and feet as he shifted.

When they sat in the car, Daron said, "That other man tried to get away, but Nicco and Angela have him cornered. By the time he realized they were following him, he was already at their half-way hub."

Ryan frowned and glanced into the mirror. "I hope he didn't hurt the woman he took from the club."

"He hauled her into the building with him." Daron said from the back seat, "Nicco suspects there are other women inside, so he and Angela are weighing their options before going in. We're supposed to be there to provide backup."

Ryan spoke over his shoulder as his foot depressed the gas pedal. "Say no more."

"So about these items … " Vikkas pointed to the bag between Daron and Dro.

Dro peeled back the zipper. "Now would be a good time to check what we have, in case we run into trouble tonight."

Following Daron's direction, they reached the building in ten minutes. Along the way, Nicco had asked them to get Bashir en route with any other personnel the royal family could make available to assist. Someone would need to organize the movement of the women when they left for their secondary target.

Ryan hoped the man they were after would tell them where they needed to head next, without trying to be a hero. After chasing shadows and mirrors for days, Ryan was running short on patience. He wondered whether Aziza would be at that location, but didn't want to get his hopes up for nothing.

The squat gray structure sat on its own lot and as they pulled in front of it, Angela met them outside under the street lights in the parking lot. She pointed behind her while she updated Daron. "I left Nicco trying some gentle persuasion to get him to say where he was headed next. Another blow or two will soften him up, but we already have an idea from what he admitted."

"How many women?" he asked.

"Five, including the woman from Encounters. Apparently, this is where they keep them until the drugs wear out of their system and they're lucid again."

"Was Aziza one … "

Angela's dark eyes were sympathetic as she said, "None of these women fit her description or resemble the photos we received."

Disappointment soured Ryan's stomach, but he reassured himself their search would not be in vain.

The headlights from two SUVs swept past them. The drivers parked a few feet away, then Bashir approached with a couple men, who resembled Jai and Vikkas. They were in the middle of introductions when Nicco strode through the door, highlighted by beams from inside the building.

He nodded to the group, then held up a set of keys and dropped them into Bashir's hand. "Glad you're here. The women need medical attention, and Jai is expecting them. We have to move now."

As they separated according to the vehicles they would be riding in, Nicco added, "Our guy inside is out of it. Let him sleep until we circle back to him. He'll need to answer some more questions."

Bashir nodded and walked into the building, followed by his companions.

As he gripped the wheel, Ryan said a prayer that when they got to their next stop, Aziza would be there. He'd be disappointed, not to mention frustrated, if they had to follow more clues. The longer she was missing, the less likely it was that they'd find her. He shook off his negative thoughts and reminded himself that he'd get the results he expected.

On the way to where the other kidnap victims were being held, Daron, Dro, Vikkas, Nicco, and Angela spoke via Daron's cellular and formulated a plan in the event that they were met with hostility.

An hour's worth of driving into the desert brought them close to a settlement with one container placed adjacent to a double-wide unit. A small brick and mortar building was in close proximity. Flashes of light cut the darkness, along with the sound of gunfire.

Ryan slowed to a crawl and switched off the lights, same as Nicco had done. The SUV ahead of him stopped, and Ryan also pulled off the road. A dark SUV was parked close to the fence.

Daron ascertained there was no one inside.

"Someone else got here before us," Nicco said, standing outside Vikkas' window. "Everybody has a helmet?" he asked, while handing him a tiny radio that crackled to life.

Angela's voice emitted from the device. "Testing. Testing."

"We're hearing you loud and clear," Vikkas replied.

They left the vehicles carrying the duffle and crept toward the containers, where the gunfire had ceased. When they came to a low fence surrounding the property, one of the unseen men caught wind of their movement and shouted in Arabic.

They came under gunfire and hunkered behind the fence until the assault subsided.

"Sounds like they have semi-automatic weapons," Ryan whispered.

"Didn't expect anything else," Daron said. "The people on this side of the world like their guns as much as we do in America."

"We need to get closer," Ryan said, "otherwise we'll be pinned down here all night and exposed when daylight comes."

"I have a plan," Daron said, beckoning Nicco closer. "Dro and I will move in on one side. Nicco and Angela will attack from the other. Vikkas, you and Ryan cover us from here until we get into position. Use whatever means necessary."

"Got it."

As they melted into the darkness, Vikkas lifted a pair of tear gas grenades from the bag on the ground between them.

"You all aren't playing." Ryan said in a hushed tone. "I can help with that. I've been told I have a good pitching arm."

"Have at it," Vikkas said, handing him one of the round containers as the gunfire started again.

Ryan kneeled to scope out the place closest to where the gunshots originated. At the next ceasefire, he backed up a few steps, released the safety lever, pulled the pin, and lobbed the grenade toward the building.

A man screamed, then sobbed as the tear gas took effect. But that didn't stop the guns' barking for long. As the night wore on the attack continued, and Ryan wondered if their supply of ammunition would ever run out. The men put up a sustained fight, shooting at them from the building.

As they returned the fire, Ryan decided that if Aziza was inside the container, he'd fight to his last breath to free her. The crimson fingers of dawn lit the sky before Nicco picked off the last man with a bullet to the forehead.

That's when they approached the container.

Chapter 16

Aziza woke to a keening cry. She raised her head, searching among the women sleeping on the floor in a cluster. None of them stirred, so the wails weren't coming from inside. Her grainy eyes attested to her lack of sleep during the night just past.

The men outside had bombarded the container, but were unsuccessful in getting inside. Apparently, the panels were reinforced. The bullet that hit Hamid entered through a section of the metal that had rusted.

At the thought of him, Aziza felt sick. One woman, who confirmed she was a nurse, bandaged his shoulder where the bullet pierced him. Thankfully, it was a flesh wound. The sight of the blood unnerved most of the females, but they didn't unravel. Fact was, they had no way out while the men continued their assault.

Aziza rested her head on her folded arms. The combined odor of anxiety and sweat was not pleasant, but she refused to be distracted. Their funk was the least of her problems.

Her stomach rumbled, reminding her that three-quarters of a day had passed since she'd eaten. Neither had any of the women, but nobody complained.

The wailing continued outside, along with gunfire. While she wondered what was happening, her heart sank. Most likely, the battle was between factions intent on capturing them. The thought depressed her, and she breathed in deeply to calm her nerves.

She had led the women into this revolt, and she would see it to the end, no matter what happened. Her mother had always told her that giving up in the middle of her struggle was never a solution. The sage advice stiffened her spine, and she inched to a sitting position.

Aziza sat still, knowing she was at risk. Especially if there was a bullet out there destined to hit her. The metal box imprisoning them might have been secure, but like her dad used to say, if you were born to hang you couldn't drown. Still, she changed position and propped herself on one elbow.

Eyes closed, she tried to separate the voices. Panic echoed from the persons speaking in Arabic. Then her ears picked up the familiar cadence of the English language.

Her heart took off at a gallop. What if the men speaking English had come to save them? Until she found herself in the middle of a horror story, being a victim of human trafficking was only a figment of Aziza's imagination. Something that made her stomach turn when she heard about such incidents on social media or watched news on television.

The enormity of what they were facing swept over her, and her grandmother's face swam before her eyes. Odd that she should think of her now, but it wasn't all that strange. Evelyn Hampton was one of Aziza's heroes. She'd been in awe of the small woman she met when she was twelve and her father first took her to Jamaica to visit. Her grandmother, a feminine version her father, had enfolded her in a hug. They stood eye to eye, but Aunt Evelyn—as everybody called her—was a powerhouse in terms of her personality. After being widowed in her thirties, she raised five sons on her own. She lived at the top of a hill in the parish of Westmoreland and to this day, Aunt Evelyn refused to move in with any of her three sons, who still lived on the island. And she was seventy-five.

When Aziza thought about the tough conditions her grandmother survived and her mantra, God helps those who help themselves, she knew quitting was not one of the choices open to her. Aside from that, she wanted to lay eyes on her family. Giving up wouldn't accomplish that wish.

She desperately wanted to know what was happening outside, but there was no way ... unless she could see through the glass paneling at the top of their prison. Whoever came up with the design knew exactly what they were doing because none of the glass had shattered. Everyone in the forty-foot housing was sealed away, as if in a tomb. Except for that rusted section near the bed Hamid occupied.

Next to her, Naima stirred and her thoughts changed direction.

"I do not think they will give up," she said. "What are we going to do?"

"What we're not going to do," Aziza hissed, "is give up."

On Naima's other side, Ahaba sniffled.

"You don't have time for that now," Naima said in a gentle voice. "We need you to focus on what's going on out there. Can you do that?"

In the haze that signaled dawn, Aziza caught the girl's nod.

"Do you understand what's being said?" Naima asked, "and why they're screeching like that?"

A few more seconds went by as Ahaba changed position and tipped her head closer to the wall. After a moment, she said, "I think the men who were trying to get us are still out there. And there are some others."

Aziza bit down on her lip to contain her impatience. She had figured that out already. "Tell us what the crying is about." She swallowed the for-heaven's-sake part of the sentence.

"One of them is saying that he is blind, the other is saying that he is not willing to die for these ... " She hesitated. "He just used a nasty word to describe us."

"We need to figure out who those other men are," Aziza whispered to Naima. "I'm hoping they are friends and not foes."

"Do you have friends on this side of the world?" Naima asked. "We are in desperate need of some right now."

The gunfire continued, punctuated by intermittent screams. A few more women raised their heads. Others sat up, wrapped their arms around their knees, and rocked backward and forward, comforting themselves.

The cot across from them creaked as Hamid stirred and groaned. His head fell back to the bed and he sobbed.

Naima looked away, because he was little more than a boy. A boy in agony, as evidenced by his continued cries. Since she hit him, things kept getting progressively worse for him. But he had made his choice. She closed the door on her sympathy and turned her attention to Ahaba.

One more burst of gunfire came before a man bellowed in Arabic.

"What is he saying?" Aziza all but yelled.

Ahaba's voice quivered, but she continued, "He said, 'I surrender.'"

Aziza smiled, then whispered, "Dear God, let their enemies be my friends."

She contained her excitement, and reached for the gun. No matter who was outside, they still needed to stay alert.

The attack on the door was nothing compared to the previous assault. Her fellow prisoners scooted toward the back and huddled together in a shivering clump.

"What are we going to do if they break down the door?" Naima asked, her eyes wild in her narrow face.

"Let's think about that bridge when we're ready to cross it."

As the pounding continued, Ahaba covered both her ears. Naima went to her side and hugged her.

Aziza positioned herself in front of the women. She was no Superwoman, but she would do what she could to protect the more vulnerable among them, especially the young girls. Yesterday evening while they waited out the men, the youngest girl, Sunita—almost a baby at ten years old—had broken down sobbing. Her tale of repeated assault, after her father sold her, made Aziza's eyes sprout tears of anger while her blood boiled.

The silence, when it descended, was almost deafening. Hamid's moaning was the only noise interrupting the early morning calm. Aziza could almost believe everybody outside had left. The lack of movement stretched her frayed nerves as she waited, for what, she didn't know.

Abdul chose that moment to start shouting.

"He is telling them how many of us are in here." Ahaba's voice reeked of desperation.

Throwing aside caution, Aziza got to her feet. Propelled by anger, she thumped Abdul's forehead and yanked the fabric back over his mouth. Leaning in close, she said, "We don't know who is out there, but you better pray to God it's your people and not mine."

His yellow-brown eyes flashed hatred, but that was the least of her concern.

She didn't know why she was warning him, but the snatches of English stirred the hope that somehow they would be delivered out of this hellhole where they'd been imprisoned for nearly a week. Her focus returned to Abdul, and she kept her voice even. "You better shut it before I punch you again."

She flexed her sore fist, then dashed back to where she left the rifle leaning against the wall. Ignoring the pain in her hand and the tension pulling at the back of her neck, she hefted the rifle.

A husky and commanding voice rang through the air. "If you can hear me, my name is Nicco Wolfe and my team and I are here to help you."

Aziza's gaze shot to Naima, who stared back at her. Then a grin split her face. She sprang to her feet but Aziza pulled her back down. "We don't know for sure he is who he says he is."

Despite her doubt, Aziza stood and took unsteady steps toward the entrance.

"Did you hear me?" he asked.

Aziza stumbled and stopped herself from retreating to the safety of the group. Instead, she threw out a dare. "How do we know you're not trying to trick us?"

"We risked our lives to free you," he yelled. "You have to trust us. Please."

"Give us a reason to open this door," she challenged.

"The royal family hired us to find you." The man's voice took on a coaxing edge. "I understand your reluctance, but we really are here to help."

Aziza glanced over her shoulder as excitement spread, and the women shot to their feet. Even Sunita stood. The hope shining from her eyes made Aziza weepy.

"Aziza, is that you?"

She frowned as her knees threatened to leave her without support. When she recovered, Aziza rushed toward the pile of metal that lay between them and the desert. Tears streamed down her face, and she could barely get her words out. "Ryan, it's me."

With the back of one hand, she wiped the tears away from her cheeks. She swallowed the wad of emotion blocking her throat, and tried again in a stronger voice. "Ryan, it's Aziza."

An unnatural pause occurred where nothing moved. She believed her heart forgot its pace, too. Then, it took off at a gallop as Ryan's smooth tenor flowed over her again, "Woman, you'd better open this door before we flatten it."

He didn't have to tell her again. She set the gun to one side and dragged one of the flimsy metal beds out of the way. While she did that, her heart tried to find an escape route from her chest.

Although he spoke to her twice, Aziza could scarcely believe Ryan stood outside. She could not conceive how it was possible that he was here in Durabia, but she didn't care. All she knew was that she needed the safety of his arms. The fact that she was wearing the same housecoat for days should have mattered, plus she hadn't showered in nearly a week.

None of that meant anything.

All she wanted was to be reunited with the man she loved.

Working together, the women cleared the doorway and Aziza pulled back the latch to fly the door open. It didn't budge.

Aziza groaned as her shoulders drooped. The rumble of disappointment spread behind her.

"It won't open," she yelled.

"Don't worry," Ryan said, "We've got you. Stand back from the door."

"You got it."

When all of them were out of range, Aziza kept hold of the AK-47 for some measure of safety. "You can come in now."

"Cover your ears," Ryan instructed.

The explosion was loud but meant little to Aziza because it would free her from the horror that escalated in the last fourteen hours.

This time, when the hinges creaked and one of them sagged, excitement flooded Aziza's body and soul. She closed her eyes for a few seconds to stay grounded.

A muscular, blond man invaded the container with a gun in his hand. One corner of his mouth tipped into a wry smile. "It's clear in here, except for the woman with the AK-47." He looked her in the eyes. "I'm Nicco. Permission to approach?"

When she nodded, he crossed the cement floor, gently took the rifle from her hands and nodded—a gesture of respect. "Thank you."

"You're welcome and thank you, too."

Kelsie reluctantly handed him Abdul's gun.

Over the Nicco's shoulder, she glimpsed Ryan. They stared at each other as he approached. She didn't dare blink, in case he was an illusion conjured by her tired brain.

When his arms closed around her, a sob worked its way up from her throat, and she buried her face in his chest. After inhaling as much of him as she could in several breaths, she cried, "They took the children, Ryan. Four little girls—you need to find all of them."

Chapter 17

Sex slaves.

Ryan's stomach turned over at the scene before him. The reality of it stole his breath, same as the pictures of the women murdered for their organs.

An array of adolescent females sat on several cots the men had arranged outside the container. The hope that lit the girls' and women's eyes far outshone their condition. When they realized they were free, they spilled outside. They blinked as the sun shimmered on the traces of dew that lingered on the blades of grass and weeds that sprouted in patches around their makeshift prison.

The police had arrived, but didn't seem overly interested in the women. Abdul and Hamid were escorted to the hospital under police guard. The Sheikh's nephew, Hassan, and one other envoy also traveled with them to ensure the men didn't disappear, or were released on bail before Vikkas could bring charges against them that would stick.

Ryan's gaze left the women and returned to the surrounding group, which included two high-ranking police officers, Daron, Dro, Nicco, Bashir, and Angela.

"This isn't finished," Ryan said while the policemen shuffled their feet, as if eager to be on their way. "What's the process for dealing with these women?"

The officers exchanged a perplexed look, then the one wearing a comb-over cleared his throat. "We have to question them and find housing, which might be difficult."

"Why should that be a problem?" Angela asked, frowning. "It's clear that a crime has been committed against these women. It's the state's responsibility to provide accommodation until they have somewhere to go."

"This isn't America." Nicco's tone was gruff. "And these two don't seem ready or willing to deal with this situation."

The uniformed men hemmed and hawed but didn't propose any feasible course of action.

Dro eased out his phone, speed-dialed, and put it to his ear. "I'll get on the line with Sheikh Kamran. He and the Sheikha will come up with something. "

"This is right up their street," Daron said. "They have a facility that should be able to accommodate at least some of the women."

An uneasy glance passed between the policemen. "We will contact our headquarters and see how we can work with you to resolve this problem."

"You had your chance," Daron said, and waved at them in a dismissive gesture. "We've got this."

A sour smile came to Ryan's lips. The world over, some people only bowed to affluence and influence. This should not be the case in a sensitive situation like this one. All the same, some kind of response was better than no response from the authorities.

His gaze drifted to Aziza. More than anything, he wanted to wrap himself around her and never let her out of his sight. She was in conversation with the Senegalese woman who sat on one side, while her arm rested over the shoulder of a young Indian girl.

Aside from bruising around Aziza's jaw, she didn't seem injured. He grinned at the thought of her holding the guards captive. He'd forgotten there was a whole other side to the woman he loved. Drake and he had rolled their eyes at her persistence, but included her in the self-defense moves they had learned during those long summer months in Evanston. Who knew that stuff would come in helpful years later? He couldn't wait to get the four-one-one on everything that happened since she disappeared, but that would be much later, when they were alone.

The last twelve hours had flown by in a blur of activity and more than anything else, he needed that down-time with his woman. When they finally got back to the hotel … his thoughts strayed to the police officers.

I am a member of the security forces.

The man in his room was the same one who interrupted their meeting at the police headquarters with the Commissioner and his assistant. He said as much to Dro.

"I wonder how many more pieces of this puzzle are still missing, Seems like no sooner do we have a handle on one thing another pops up, like the guy in my room."

"We'll have answers soon enough," Dro said. "The room attendant checked out, but Daron placed a bug in the housekeeping department to keep an eye and ear on things. Just in case."

Ryan nodded and swallowed a yawn. He was dead tired. Earlier, he was shaken to his core to see the actual result of a wholesale trafficking operation. Modern day slavery. How many women had been taken and never saw their family again? How long had this ring been in existence, and why didn't the police pay more attention to what was a growing problem?

After Daron spoke to Sheik Kamran, Sheikha Ellena sent a team of medical personnel to do preliminary checks on the rescued group. Bashir proved helpful with crossing the language barrier on both sides.

Jai had a team of doctors, nurses, and mental health professionals, including Blair Ali Khan, Chaz Maharaj and Ahmad Maharaj waiting at his medical facility.

Aziza's gaze clung to his, and Ryan gave her what he hoped was an encouraging smile. He wanted the business end of things wrapped up within the next twenty minutes. He could almost believe they had been standing around for half a day as the early morning chill dissipated and the sun gained ascendancy.

As if God heard his unspoken prayer, two passenger vehicles trundled over the sand toward them. Two men climbed out of each van. After greeting them, one driver announced, "His Royal Highness,

Sheikh Kamran Ali Khan and Sheikha Ellena sent us to pick up the passengers."

Ryan walked away and held out his hand to Aziza. She held on to his fingers, then allowed him to slip one arm around her. "You're coming with me," he said.

Aziza inclined her head toward the others. "Where are they going?"

"The Sheikh's wife has a facility where they can stay." He touched her jaw. "At this point, I'm not sure I'll ever let you out of my sight again. Ever."

Laying both hands on his chest, Aziza murmured, "I'd love to travel with you, but it's better if I stay with them. For now."

As if the little girl sensed a separation was coming, she hurried to where Aziza stood and grabbed a handful of her dress. One by one, the women came to stand with Aziza and the child.

From his position next to Aziza, Ryan looked deep into her eyes. This woman had so much more to her personality than he knew or appreciated. Adversity had a way of bringing out the best and worst in people. Although she could have had the advantage of travelling with him in privacy and comfort, she chose to remain with the others.

Ryan pressed his lips to her forehead. "As long as I know you're safe, I'll be all right."

He clasped her hand, and after a few seconds she tugged at him. A mischievous light shone from her eyes. "Though we're not dressed for polite company, and might smell a little ripe, I'm sure it would be okay if you ride with us."

Ryan grinned back at her. "That's the best invitation I've had all day."

Chapter 18

Aziza couldn't stop touching Ryan. As soon as her hands rested in her lap, one of them strayed to settle on his thigh. When he squeezed her hand, she gave up pretending. She'd never been a clinging vine, hanging on to her man, but after the experiences of the past week, she was under no illusion about her need for this man. His solid presence was a constant reminder that her ordeal was over, that she was safe. Sighing, she leaned her head on his shoulder.

She was the last of the fifteen women to undergo an examination because she couldn't tear herself away from him. And as sour as she was after days of not showering, Ryan hadn't left her side. Now that was some straight up love right there.

Aziza had just finished talking with her mother in a tearful reunion on his cell phone when a nurse called her name and beckoned her forward.

Ryan rose with her and went as far as the door of the examination room.

The female doctor introduced herself, then conducted a thorough exam which took some time. Earlier, a nurse collected blood and a urine sample for testing. While the doctor gently poked and prodded Aziza, her gaze swept around the high-tech, silver-and-grey facility. Keeping her mind occupied meant ignoring the silly tears that sprang to her eyes for no good reason.

After allowing her to pull on a clean hospital gown and step into a pair of slippers, the motherly woman said, "I don't see any signs of sexual activity. Does that mean you were not molested?"

"Thank God, no." Aziza said, then sighed on remembering ten-year-old Sunita.

Her story was enough to make an adult weep. How a man could find a prepubescent child attractive was a mystery to Aziza. Sunita was still a baby and needed protection.

"I know about patient confidentiality and all that, but the little girl you examined just before me, will she be okay? Physically, I mean. I only ask because I've been taking care of her."

She stared at Aziza, then her lips twisted. "I will tell you because it's clear to me that you are concerned … in a good way. She has been sexually molested, but seems to be healthy. The tests will say for certain."

"Thank you," Aziza whispered. "I appreciate you for telling me."

The doctor nodded. "I am a mother, so I understand how you feel. Take care of her."

Nodding, Aziza said, "I will."

On her return to the secure waiting area designated for the group, Aziza sat next to the girl, who slipped her hand into hers. Her stringy hair and sad, yet hopeful eyes made Aziza want to do whatever it would take to bring a smile to her face.

Close to the doorway, the woman Ryan introduced as Angela stood with her back facing them. She wore the same combat gear as the men and was part of a conversation taking place outside the room. Every so often, she looked over her shoulder as if to reassure herself they were all right.

When she stepped out of the doorway, two women walked inside. One of them was a tall, Black woman with a low Afro and the other was a tiny, Asian woman.

Angela, though fierce in all black, wore a warm smile. "Ladies, meet Rae." She pointed to the African-American female. "And this is Linda. These ladies will take care of you."

Instead of being excited, the newly released women huddled closer together on the benches, the soup in their hands forgotten.

Rae and Linda shared a glance, then Rae addressed them with both hands open. "Our circumstances may be different, but we, too, have had our challenges. I know it's hard to trust anybody right now, but you'll see that we are here to help. Nothing else."

Linda nodded, then waved toward the door. "If you can't trust us, let me reassure you that you can trust this lady right here."

A stately woman wearing cream linen walked into the room. Her honey-gold skin glowed with good health and her serene smile encouraged confidence. She nodded to acknowledge Rae and Linda, then addressed the disheveled group. "I'm Amanda Maharaj, and you will be my guests for the next few days while we come up with a plan. In that time, you can decide if you wish to return home or remain in Durabia."

She clasped both hands in front of her and continued, "We know you've been through a lot, but bear with us. Now, it's time for us to transport you to your accommodations."

They breathed a collective sigh, then got to their feet, but Sunita stayed next to Aziza and gripped her hand tighter. Giving the child a reassuring smile, Aziza murmured, "Don't worry. You'll be all right."

Ryan appeared in the doorway, followed by Daron and Dro, whom he'd introduced earlier. He explained that they were Kings of the Castle, brothers to Shaz. The mention of Shaz's name was enough for Aziza. The men now stood against the wall as the women filed out of the holding area.

Brothers? They must all come from different mothers.

Sunita didn't leave Aziza's side. In front of them, the small Asian woman waited patiently while Aziza cupped Sunita's cheek and looked her in the eyes. "I know you don't want to go, but I'll come and see you later in the day, okay?"

She stared back at Aziza for a few seconds before nodding. Still, she didn't get to her feet.

As Ryan approached, an idea came to Aziza. She held out a hand to him."D'you have paper and a pen?"

"Sure." He pulled a folded sheet of paper from the protective vest he wore. He made a seam and tore off the bottom edge of the notepaper. Then he removed a pen from one of the leg pockets in his pants and held both toward her.

"Are you using the same telephone number here?" Aziza asked.

"Yeah, but—"

Aziza scribbled his contact information and wrote both their names. "I'm giving it to Sunita, so she can call me." She smiled at the little girl. "Is that okay, baby?"

She nodded, and her eyes sparkled.

Aziza tapped her under the chin and gave her the paper. "See you in a while, okay?"

Sunita released her and left with Linda.

When she was out of sight, Aziza rested against the wall and let out her breath.

"You okay?" Ryan asked, sitting next to her.

"I'm right as rain, but need a bed, a shower, and maybe a little shut-eye."

"That doesn't sound too hard." Ryan stood and helped her up by the elbow. His fingers surrounded her arm as a prolonged wail cut through the air.

"What the hell?" Ryan propelled her forward with him, and they rushed to the doorway.

A solid force knocked the air out of Aziza, who instinctively put out her arms and encircled the human dynamo that crashed into her stomach.

Sunita sobbed with her face buried in Aziza's dress and squeezed her tight. "What's the matter?" she asked, alarmed. She stroked Sunita's hair while her heart beat at the pace of runaway racehorse.

Linda frowned as she rushed up to them. "I'm not sure what just happened—"

"I think I do," Ryan said, as he sped through the entrance of the health center.

Chapter 19

The doctor's flapping coattail directed Ryan to the corner of the building where he disappeared.

Ryan increased his pace, sprinting down the pathway behind the man, who looked to be half his height. Footsteps beat a path behind him, and he figured Daron and Dro were on their trail. They had been standing outside the building with the women when Sunita cried out. He hated to think about what her distress meant, but he already knew.

The man rounded the corner.

Ryan followed, lengthened his stride, and tackled the runner.

"Uggghhhh."

They landed on the ground, and the doctor struggled to get from under Ryan's weight. He spoke in his ear. "If you know what's good for you, you'll stop wriggling around. Now."

As soon as the doctor went still, Ryan stood and hauled the portly man to his feet. Daron, Dro, Nicco, and Angela stood around them. Eluding all of them would have been impossible.

"Why are you in such a hurry?" Ryan's gaze went to the man's chest, where his name was embroidered on his coat. "Dr. Butala."

Now that they faced each other, Ryan swept the man from head to feet—bulbous nose, wispy hair styled into a comb-over, thick hands with blunt fingers, and his tie askew. He had been tidy before Ryan landed on top of him and messed up his clothes.

Glaring at him, Dr. Butala straightened his glasses and dusted his grimy coat. In a thick accent he said, "You were chasing me."

"Yeah, but that came after the sight of you frightened that little girl."

Dr. Butala blinked once. "I am sure you are mistaken."

Arms across his chest, Ryan said, "I know what I saw. That child is terrified of you. I need to know why."

A film of sweat covered the doctor's forehead, and he swiped his face with the back of his sleeve. His gaze swept the group as if seeking a means of escape.

Ryan scanned the well-kept garden behind them as the doctor protested. "I have patients to see, and I do not understand why you have attacked me in my place of work. I will report this to the administrator."

"There's no need." Daron said, waving one hand. "Here he comes now."

Ryan had not met Jai Maharaj other than on a computer screen and did a double take when he laid eyes on the tall replica of Vikkas. The only thing that differentiated the two was the sliver of white hair in Jai's widow's peak.

"Dr. Butala," Jai said, nodding at Ryan. "We should take this inside."

"I—I have patients to see." He tipped his chin into the air and gave Ryan a killing glare. "Can we meet later?"

"As you well know, this facility is fully staffed. I will assign someone to see your patients until we sort out this matter. I'm certain this won't take long."

As Dr. Butala's eyes flickered, Ryan's stomach shriveled. This would be bad. He sensed that rather than this case winding down, they had barely scratched the peak of the iceberg.

"We cannot take him back inside past Sunita," Ryan said. "Can we use a different entrance?"

Jai nodded and pointed the group toward a parking garage a few feet away.

"I'll go check with Aziza and see if she found out exactly what happened to Sunita."

"While you're doing that," Dro said, motioning to Nicco. "We'll take care of this matter."

He escorted Dr. Butala down the walkway, leaving Daron to re-introduce Ryan and Jai.

"This will be interesting," Jai said. "No matter how often we clean house, there's always some rubbish left behind."

Daron squeezed his shoulder. "You did the best you could with what you had at the time. You've done well considering that you're even operating this facility in a place steeped in tradition."

"Right, but I will not allow this bit of scum to cause me to lose everything I've worked for in this country." He shoved both hands into his pockets and set his jaw. "If Dr. Butala has touched any of the women or children in his care, I will kill him with my bare hands and none of you can stop me."

Daron nodded slowly as Jai stalked toward the back of the clinic.

Ryan figured there was some history of which he was not aware, but of course, now wasn't the time to ask.

"See you in Jai's office in a few minutes." Daron said.

They went to the front of the building, where they parted company.

Aziza sat in the private waiting area where Ryan had kept her company earlier. She looked up when he entered the room, still stroking Sunita's hair. The little girl had fallen asleep with her head resting on Aziza's lap.

The welcoming light in her eyes made Ryan smile. Even in the hospital gown, she was beautiful. He sat next to her, and her head came to rest in the crook of his neck.

"Did Sunita tell you what frightened her?" he asked, smoothing the skin on Aziza's arm.

"From what I pieced together, he abused her ... repeatedly." Tears filled Aziza's eyes as she continued, "I gather she was in some kind of place where there were girls of all ages. She called it *El Zalaam*.

I couldn't get the poor baby to stop screaming. She was sure he was coming to get her."

"Well, we know that won't happen," Ryan said, seething with disgust.

A nurse went past the door as Aziza asked, "How did you know what the problem was?"

"My training in the police force. A child doesn't behave like that for no reason. And a grown man doesn't take off running, unless he's in danger or scared. I've learned to be more observant than the ordinary man."

"So where is that ... that ... " Her eyes flashed heat. "I can't even find a word to describe him."

"Jai—the owner of this facility—will investigate. Dro and Nicco are with him, so there's no fear of him escaping.

Aziza released a long sigh. "I feel as if I've already lived thirty-six hours today."

"The hotel isn't far, and we'll soon be finished here. Just a little while longer, babe."

Aziza shifted and cupped his jaw. "Do you mind if Sunita stays with us?"

"If it's okay with Mrs. Maharaj, then it's okay with me." His gaze settled on Sunita. "Though I'm not sure if, by law, she's supposed to be anywhere else but under the government's care."

Aziza set her jaw, and her stare did not waver.

He knew what that meant. After what Aziza had been through, he didn't want to give her a moment's stress. "I'll find out what papers we have to sign to get temporary custody of her."

"Thanks, love." The admiration in her eyes made him want to do somersaults and undertake bigger exploits. For now, he'd have the necessary conversations to give Aziza the assurance she craved.

"Where are the others? Did they leave?" he asked.

"The first van left, and the other one loaded up while you were chasing that bit of slime." She grabbed his wrist and looked him dead in the eyes. "I want to be sure they get to their destination safely," she said.

"It's not that I don't trust your people. But after what we went through ... we need to call later."

Ryan kissed her cheek, then got to his feet. "We'll do that. Be back in a few."

He went to the intake counter and asked for directions to Jai Maharaj's office. The nurse asked an attendant to escort him to a secluded corner of the complex. After he rapped on the door, Jai invited him to come inside. He introduced him to a tall man he'd apparently been meeting with before things went awry.

"Ryan, this is Chaz Maharaj. He also works here at the clinic."

Although he didn't mention that they were relatives, their resemblance was close enough for Ryan to believe he'd made an accurate guess.

At Jai's invitation, Ryan sat next to Chaz in front of the desk.

Dr. Butala, who cowered in an adjacent seat, seemed to have shrunk in size since their run-in. The antique chair he sat in dwarfed him. Despite the air-conditioning, he was sweating, and his darting eyes wouldn't settle anywhere.

"All of this is unnecessary," Dr. Butala said. "I have told you several times, I do not know that little girl and even if I have visited *El Zalaam*, it is legal to do so."

"And you should be ashamed of yourself," Jai snapped. "To be treating young females when you know perfectly well you have a fetish. I repeatedly told the Durabia Tribunal I did not want to hire you. If I find out from any of the patients, or the nurses, that you touched any of them in inappropriate ways, I *will* have you thrown in prison."

The man sat up and gripped both chair arms. "But I am a national. And it is also legal—"

"Be careful what you say to me." Jai's eyes narrowed. "I hold my staff to stricter standards than any other hospital in Durabia. You signed a contract agreeing to certain conditions, so I have every right to ensure you abide by the stipulations in that document."

Dr. Butala's olive skin blanched, and he shifted in the chair. "None of my patients will have complaints."

"That had better be the case." Jai pointed at him. "And if I find out you've been threatening any of them. I won't be as lenient with you as the law might be."

"What happens if there's proof he's been messing with these little girls?" Ryan spared the doctor a scathing glance. "Aziza confirmed that Sunita knows him."

"I wouldn't want to put her through the trauma of having to face him in court," Jai said, "Which is why I will give Dr. Butala an hour to get his things and be prepared for the Kings to handle him."

The doctor's eyes bulged. "But—"

"You do *not* want to cross me." Jai's face was set in grim lines. "Just be thankful you didn't touch her on the hospital grounds, or you'd be leaving in handcuffs."

The man stood as if someone had set a fire under him. "You are treating me unfairly on the words of a little ..."

He attached an Arabic word that shocked both Chaz and Jai, who shoved away his chair and shot to his feet. "It's best if you walk out of here now, while you still can, rather than me sending you out on a stretcher."

Ryan stifled a grin behind his hand. For someone who seemed mild-mannered at first glance, Jai had a smoldering volcano inside him. He picked up the handset and jabbed a button. "Please have security escort Dr. Butala to his locker. I'll arrange for him to be removed from the premises."

"You might live to regret this," Dr. Butala said, his tone fierce. "Remember, I am the most recognized thoracic and gastrointestinal surgeon in Durabia."

His declaration raised Ryan's antenna. If this man was perverted enough to objectify children sexually, how far-fetched was it that he might also be involved in slicing and dicing women for profit?

Dro, who had been using a tablet, looked up again and lowered the device.

Daron leaned off the wall and put both hands in his pockets. "I suggest you do not allow your mouth to write any checks the rest of your body can't cash."

Dr. Butala's bulbous nose twitched, but he didn't say another word.

A knock on the door interrupted the tense silence. On Jai's command, a distinguished man wearing a suit and turban entered the office, greeted them, then left with the doctor.

As soon as the door closed, Ryan sat forward, "Based on what the distinguished doctor said, it isn't a stretch to think he might be involved in organ harvesting. I'm just saying."

"I get that, and it bears looking into for sure." Jai sighed and leaned back in his seat. "In case you're wondering why I hired Dr. Butala—"

"I'm not blaming you for anything," Ryan rushed to say. "A crafty individual will show you the persona they think you will approve of at a job interview. It's human nature."

"And it doesn't help that the laws of the land require me to hire twenty percent nationals, which is how this substandard fool ended up at this clinic—against my wishes." He lapsed into silence, then looked directly at Chaz. "Kamran is having a challenging time trying to compromise with the old guard. But this right here is not going to fly."

He tapped the desk hard. "This facility and my license will be in jeopardy if this gets out. We've already come through a harrowing experience in the States, and this clinic will *not* be part of any scandal in Durabia."

His words hung in the silence as the men absorbed them, then made sounds of agreement.

"On another note," Ryan said, "Aziza would like Sunita to stay with us. Is that something you can arrange, or do we have to ask Ms. Maharaj?"

Jai gave him a serene smile and pulled his laptop closer. "Under the circumstances and from a medical point of view, I can give you a certificate to release her into Aziza's care, since she seems to be the only person she trusts."

"I really appreciate that," Ryan said, then let his attention shift to Daron and Dro, who were as comfortable in business suits as the paramilitary gear they now wore. "Are we ready to go?"

"We have some Castle business to discuss and palace business, too" Daron said.

Dro looked up from his tablet. "I know you're happy and all, but don't forget this isn't over. The Sheikh has charged us with destroying this trafficking ring, and we still have to find those girls. In the meantime, we've put together another unit, including Hassan, who you've already met, plus Calvin and Rahm, to continue following their trail. So enjoy your time with your lady, but in the morning you belong to us."

Ryan grinned as the printer on the credenza behind Jai whirred to life and spat out a sheet of paper.

Jai affixed his signature, folded the document, and put it into an envelope. "This should be good if anyone asks questions."

"Appreciate it." Ryan saluted them and turned to go. "Catch you later and thanks for everything."

Dro closed the cover on the tablet and nodded once. "Being family to Shaz makes you family to us."

Ryan bobbed his head in response and left the room. Although they had only been working together for close to a week, it felt good to be in a team where every part fit seamlessly. God knew he was grateful. This morning's operation could have turned out differently.

Now, it was time to make up ground with his woman and do what he should have done before she disappeared.

Chapter 20

The well-dressed brunette, and the man with her, rushed to Ryan's side before Aziza could warn him. The reporter stuck a recording device in his face. "Sir, can you tell me anything about the women who were reportedly kidnapped?"

Ryan slid behind the wheel, fired up the engine, then said, "No comment."

Aziza held her breath, hoping the woman would ignore her presence by some miracle.

Her focus shifted to Sunita in the backseat. She'd curled up and gone back to sleep the moment she lay on the seat. Poor thing probably hadn't enjoyed a good night's rest in months. One good piece of news Aziza received at the hospital was that Sunita was free of disease.

The brunette leaned forward and spoke through the window. "Miss, do you have a comment?"

Staring straight ahead, Aziza said, "No."

"Excuse me," Ryan had the courtesy to say as he backed the vehicle out of the parking spot.

The woman trotted alongside the vehicle with the cameraman hovering next to her. "Why are you and the little girl wearing the same clothing?"

"Because we're coming from the hospital," Aziza snapped.

The sunlight reflected off the asphalt, giving her an immediate headache.

"Don't engage her," Ryan growled through the corner of his mouth.

The cameraman moved swiftly to Aziza's side of the vehicle with his equipment ready to shoot.

Aziza lowered her head into her lap, as Ryan peeled out of the grounds.

A moment later, he laid a hand on her back. "You can sit up now."

She did, sighing with exhaustion. After a couple of minutes, she couldn't keep her eyes open. The past twenty-four hours were catching up with her. When her head snapped forward and back, Ryan gently squeezed her leg. "You can have some shut-eye until we get to the hotel."

She yawned and laid her head against the seat. "I wonder how they knew about what happened to us."

Ryan shrugged. "The police know and every police department has a leak. I'm sure this isn't the first time the clinic is seeing this type of activity. Don't worry about it."

Raising her head, Aziza asked, "What if they're waiting for us when we get to the hotel?"

"You really need some sleep," Ryan said. "How will they know where we're going, especially since we have a head start?"

She laughed, a soft throaty sound. "You win this time, but if I have a welcoming committee at the hotel, you will not hear the end of it."

He stroked her cheek and met her gaze for a second. "Like I said, I got you."

She sighed and closed her eyes.

When they arrived at the hotel ten minutes later, she woke the moment he touched her shoulder. "We're here, Zee." She sat up to find he now stood outside the passenger door. "You will have to help me. I feel a little weak."

After the slop she'd eaten the entire week, and despite the soup she drank at the hospital, she still felt she was running on empty. Ryan assisted her onto the asphalt and after making sure she could stand on her own, he opened the back door. "You should wake her up."

Aziza sat and gently shook Sunita by the shoulder. "Come on, sweetie, it's time to go inside."

Sunita sat up, rubbing her eyes. Before they were fully open, she swung her head to both sides as if trying to figure out her location. Her skinny frame sagged when she recognized Aziza, who gave her a reassuring smile,

"Everything's okay," Aziza whispered.

She climbed out of the car with Sunita clutching her hand too tight. Aziza imagined how imposing the front of the hotel must have looked to the girl, who had been locked up for months.

After parking the car, Ryan walked into the hotel as if he owned the place and like he wasn't wearing tactical gear, minus a helmet. Although he caught a few eyes, people were more interested in Aziza and Sunita.

Aziza tipped her chin up and did not make eye contact with anyone.

As though attuned to her discomfort, Ryan reached for her hand, and she allowed him to fold her fingers in his warm grip. He drew her closer. "We'll be upstairs in a minute. I'll come back down and do the necessaries later."

The elevator came in seconds, and she couldn't help being relieved that it was empty. She hoped it stayed that way until they arrived at Ryan's floor.

Aziza got her wish, and minutes later they walked down a carpeted corridor to Ryan's room. As he let them in, he said, "The Sheikh has treated me like royalty, so we have a suite."

She glanced at Sunita. "Thank God for that."

The living area, decorated in cream, gold, and touches of silver was elegant with heavy sofas loaded under plump cushions. The drapery was pulled back from the windows, letting in light and giving the impression of even more space. Aziza was more than grateful to exchange her previous meager confines for this luxurious space..

Sunita stood by her side, as if afraid to touch anything.

"You can sit, sweetie." Aziza accompanied her words with an encouraging smile. To Ryan, she said, "The first thing we need is a shower. After that, we can think about food and clothing."

"I'll get room service," he said, reaching for the dining card on the center table. "Fancy anything in particular?"

"Nope, I'm so grateful to be out of that prison, even a hamburger would do."

"Leave it to me. You ladies can take care of your needs while I organize our dinner."

"Where's your comb?" she asked.

"Huh?"

"We're going to need one in a few minutes."

"Sure, they're in the bathroom. I'll call housekeeping and have them send up some extra toiletries."

"Thanks, love." In that moment, Aziza was so grateful for that small favour, she almost burst into tears. She rested a hand on her chest and swallowed hard to get a grip on her emotions.

Ryan watched her, his face radiating affection and tenderness.

When her eyes filled again, Aziza looked away and motioned to Sunita. They both made a beeline for the bedroom and the bathroom, which was the size of a small living room. The jacuzzi was something out of an upscale home and gardening magazine, and large enough for a small child to swim. The beige-and-brown tiles and gold fittings provided an elegant backdrop for a relaxing self-care experience. But that could wait.

Given Sunita's history, Aziza was cautious about how she introduced the idea of a bath.

Sunita's eyes were wide with wonder as she ran one small hand over the edge of the bath.

Pointing to her right, Aziza said, "We can use the shower if you prefer."

With a vigorous nod, Sunita settled that matter.

"Will you let me wash your hair?" Aziza asked.

Again, Sunita nodded but didn't move to get inside the stall, shielded by glass. She hunched and stepped back, twisting her fingers together.

Aziza kneeled in front her, sensing what was wrong. "I won't hurt you. All we're going to do is wash your hair, then allow you to bathe, okay?"

Going on instinct, Aziza rose and pulled the dress over her head. She let it fall to the floor and, wearing her undies, stepped into the granite enclosure. While she selected the shampoo from among the hotel personal care samples, Sunita removed her dress and walked inside.

Aziza turned on the tap and frowned when no water emerged. She twisted another nozzle and water hit her from three directions, plus the showerhead. Aziza let out a squeak and tried to dodge the water. Her frantic clawing at the gold spigot amused Sunita, who laughed for the first time since they met.

When Aziza finally got the pipe turned off, she chuckled. "That's not funny."

Sunita laughed again. "Yes, it is, Auntie."

Aziza beckoned to her. "Now that I know how these pipes work, let's wash your hair."

She shampooed, conditioned, and detangled Sunita's hair, then allowed her to soap and rinse herself. When she wrapped a fluffy towel around the girl and another around her head like a turban, Aziza chuckled. "You look like a queen."

A grin broke over Sunita's face and snatched Aziza's breath. She deserved this moment of laughter and all the good things life had not afforded her as yet. Aziza used another few minutes to gather Sunita's hair into two plaits, and told her that she would return in a moment. On her way out, she wrapped a robe around herself.

Ryan met her outside the bedroom door and handed her a container of personal items. "Everything all right?" he asked.

"Thanks, that was quick," she said. "Can I borrow two tee-shirts?"

"They're hanging in the cupboard. Take whatever you want."

She smiled, tipping her head to one side. "I hope you remember those words when I ask you for something bigger."

He rose and came to her. After dropping a kiss on her forehead, he murmured, "Nothing will ever be too hard, or big, for me to do for you."

A lump rose in her throat, and her eyes smarted. "Thank you," she whispered.

Ryan wore an enigmatic smile, but even without declaring his heart with words, Aziza knew this man loved her. No way would he leave his comfortable existence in what amounted to Paradise to chase someone halfway around the world if he didn't. *He could have considered me dead and forgotten about me, but thank God he's persistent.*

She sent up a brief prayer for the women. If they were lucky, they could rest without having nightmares. And hopefully, the men that had been assigned to do the job would find those girls. She took the shirts and hurried back to Sunita, who stood in front of the dresser reaching into the bowl of soap bars in gold wrapping.

The girl pulled her hand back as if guilty of stealing, or something worse.

"It's okay. Nobody will punish you for being curious." Aziza held out a pale-blue tee. "Put this on, then brush your teeth."

She did, and they both giggled at the sight she made in the full-length mirror. Ryan's shirt caught her mid-calf.

"Don't worry," Aziza said, "When I'm finished, we'll go downstairs when and get some clothes that fit. Stay with Ryan while I shower."

The light in Sunita's eyes dimmed, and her smile faded.

"Are you afraid of Ryan?"

Sunita's head jerked toward the living room then back to Aziza, but she didn't answer.

"Ryan won't harm you. He's one of the good guys." Aziza leaned toward her, unsure if Sunita understood her words. She tried again. "I want you to be comfortable and that's not possible if you just stand here while I shower. If you prefer, you can stay right there, by the door until I finish, okay? But it also makes me feel better if an adult is watching you while I can't. Do you understand?"

Although Sunita nodded, doubt shrouded the atmosphere around her. While she brushed her teeth, Aziza did the same. Then, with a hand on her shoulder, Aziza led Sunita to the living room where Ryan sat in front of his laptop.

"Can you watch Sunita while I shower?"

"Sure." He switched on the television, found a channel showing an animated film, then held out the remote to the child. "Here you go."

Sunita took the control, settled on the seat closest to the bedroom, and gave Aziza an anemic smile.

A pang of sadness shot through Aziza at the thought of Sunita's age. Maybe she'd be able to forget some of the horrors she'd been through. At this point, only God knew if her experiences hadn't scarred her for life. With any luck, they could find a welcoming family and get her re-settled.

Though she hadn't been able to speak to Ryan privately at the time, the team of men who had worked tirelessly impressed her. She meant nothing to any of them. But Shaz ... she'd be grateful to him for life. Ryan had told her of their exchange that put him on a plane to Durabia. In fact, if she ever had any kids, she'd ask Shaz to be godfather to at least one of them.

All these thoughts ran through her head as she washed her hair, which was a rat's nest of wild curls. Her mind flashed back to their time on Paradise Island, which seemed so far away. The idyllic days and passionate nights filled her memory. Ryan was definitely a keeper, and she couldn't help wishing they wouldn't be separated again. Ever.

She rinsed her undies, then stepped out of the shower and into one of Ryan's jocks. In front of the mirror, she smiled at her reflection. The weird thing was, she didn't care about her appearance. Life was so much more precious than wasting her time worrying about being seen in her man's small clothes. All the same, since she had to go out, she'd borrow one of his sweat bottoms. While she tamed her hair, Aziza grinned into the bevel edged mirror.

Freedom was priceless.

She stepped through the bedroom door and instead of sitting where she left her, Sunita sat cross-legged beside the doorway. Rather than chiding her, Aziza held out a hand, which Sunita grasped and came to her feet on the carpet.

Ryan met Aziza's gaze, and his tiny shrug said everything.

"Let's have something to eat," she said, moving to the table where a tray of fruits waited.

She put a couple of pineapple slices on a plate, then watched Sunita copy her actions.

The little girl closed her eyes as she bit into a strawberry.

"How long before the food gets here, Ryan?"

"Another few minutes."

"We need to run downstairs to get some things. D'you mind?"

"Are you sure you don't want me to go and get what you need?" His attention shifted to his underwear and her bare feet. He bit one corner of his lips. "Just tell me what to buy."

"Thanks, but it's better if I go. You won't know what to get for Sunita. I did plan to borrow one of your sweat bottoms."

"Be my guest, but there's something we have to do first."

"What's that?"

He lowered the cover of the laptop, gripped her wrist, and stood. "Come with me. You too, Sunita."

When they stood on the balcony, Ryan took Aziza's hand and held out the other to Sunita. She looked at it for several seconds before she put hers into his open one.

His attention went beyond them to the land spread out below. Hanan was a picturesque city, and she could well understand Ryan's fascination. His gaze came back to her and travelled over her face, down her body to her feet and back. While he studied her in minute detail, Aziza couldn't miss the appreciation in his gaze. He smiled, then closed his eyes and thanked God for His goodness, for keeping her safe, and returning her and Sunita. When he finished, Aziza added to his prayer with a soft appeal. "Father, we ask You to show us where those four girls are hidden. They don't deserve what's happening to them. Give Ryan and the Kings the wisdom they need to rescue them. We thank You for this victory."

She let the tension drain from her body, then whispered, "Amen."

"That means we agree with his prayer," she said, tightening her grip on Sunita.

The girl nodded as if she understood. "Amen."

Ryan grinned at her. "That's it, baby girl."

Sunita gave him a tentative smile before he led them inside and picked up his wallet off the table. He pulled out a credit card, handed it to Aziza, and reeled off the PIN. "Use this."

As her heart warmed all over again, she whispered, "Thank you."

His nod and affectionate gaze said everything.

God, she loved this man.

Chapter 21

Ryan had tasted heaven and hoped hell stayed at bay, but he remained on edge.

Dinner felt like Christmas, with Zee within arm's reach and Sunita eating until he thought she'd pop. She fell asleep at the table with one of her pigtails resting on the edge of her plate. Good thing she was already wearing the pajamas Aziza bought earlier.

Aziza created a snug haven for Sunita on a pull-out bed. When he laid her down, she didn't stir. They stood looking down at the little girl, and Ryan conjured a picture of what their future might look like. As if his thoughts filtered to her, Aziza faced him and wrapped both arms around his waist.

"She's a cute little thing," he said.

With a soft snicker, Aziza said, "Are you thinking the same thing as I am?"

"That maybe we should have a little Sunita or two of our own?"

Her arms crept up to circle his neck. "Something like that," she whispered as their lips met.

Earlier, he ordered a bottle of champagne, which he stashed in the fridge. Now was a good time to tell Aziza how he felt about her and cement his plans.

His phone vibrated and he knew this slice of nirvana was at an end.

Ryan stole one last kiss and groaned as he pulled away from Aziza. "I have to answer that."

With one finger, she trailed a line down his chest. "Get it and let's continue from where we stopped."

Ryan picked up the cellular off the center table, frowning. Everything in him said their time together was over.

Dro was on the other end. "I know I said you had tonight, but something's come up."

He sat while Aziza secured the blanket around Sunita and switched on a lamp in that corner of the room. Ryan waited for the news Dro called to deliver, hoping it wasn't what he'd guessed. "I hope it isn't what I'm thinking."

"It may very well be," Dro said. "The first passenger van didn't make it to the women's center."

"That's ... " He rubbed the back of his neck. At least, now he knew why he sensed something was wrong. "Do we know anything?"

His sharp tone startled Aziza, who stared at him, then sank next to him.

"They had a flat and apparently in the time it took to reach them, someone hijacked them. According to the staff, their attackers loaded the women into another vehicle and headed toward Nadaum."

He lowered his head. "Jesus."

Aziza tugged at his sleeve, forcing him to look at her.

"In a minute," he mouthed. Addressing Dro, he asked, "D'you have any idea where they might have taken them?"

"That is why we need you. Nicco and Angela are on site with the police. They will collect all the important details. We need to circle back to the warehouse. Meet me downstairs in ten."

"Sure."

The silence in the room settled around them, while Ryan thought about the irony of the situation. What they spent a week bringing to completion was undone in minutes.

"You're leaving, aren't you?" Aziza said, gripping his arm.

"Yeah, we have a situation."

Anxiety shadowed her eyes as she asked, "Does it have anything to do with the women today?"

He considered lying so she wouldn't worry, but didn't. That would only delay the inevitable and ruin her trust in him. "Some of them didn't make it to the shelter."

"How could that happen? It's like no one can be trusted in this godforsaken place. I knew we should have called, but with everything else I forgot." She stood with him, then paced the room as if trying to find a solution to this fresh problem. After a few seconds, she stopped abruptly. "I have a thing or two to say to Akbar. I feel he knows something about who drugged me."

Ryan stopped her with both hands on her shoulders. "Listen to me, while I'm gone you have to take care of that little girl over there. Your safety is my priority. Don't go chasing after anybody unless I'm here to back you up."

A sour expression came over her face, but he persisted. "Promise me you won't leave this suite until I return."

She tipped her head back. "Not even if I need to get anything? I still have accommodations close by, you know."

His tone was gentle, but serious when he said, "Do *not* go anywhere."

"I won't." She rolled her eyes. "I'll wait here like a docile little woman until you finish your business."

They engaged in a silent battle of wills until Aziza sighed. "I'm sorry, that was selfish of me. Go find those women. And don't forget those four girls. I'll stay here like you asked."

"Thank you." He pulled her into a hug and breathed in a lungful of tangerine essence from her hair. "I'll be back as soon as I can."

They separated, and he stalked to the bedroom closet to gather the gear he'd need. He stripped off the garments he wore and pulled on black corduroys and a black tee-shirt. He laced up his boots, then unlocked the safe and got out his Beretta 92FS which he slipped into an ankle holster. The protective vest was the last piece needed to complete his outfit.

Aziza leaned in the doorway watching him and stood straight when he approached her. He pressed his lips to hers, eased her mouth open, and caressed her tongue with his. She whimpered as he drank his fill, as if he'd never see her again.

"Don't go anywhere," he said, stroking her cheek.

She nodded, her eyes hazy. "I'll try to get some rest while you're gone, and I'll be praying for you."

"Thank you."

She walked him to the door, where he hugged her again. They stood motionless for several seconds, staring at each other.

"Be safe," she whispered.

"We have unfinished business, so I'll definitely be back."

On his way downstairs in the elevator, Ryan thought about how many things could turn around in a day.

Dro waited for him in the lobby and in no time, they sat inside the Limo.

"You've taken to driving this Limo like a pro," Dro said.

Ryan chuckled as he exited the hotel property. "I'm a quick learner."

After a moment he asked, "Where exactly are we meeting Daron?"

"He and Bashir went back to the warehouse. Daron is pulling information from their phones to cross-reference the information from the men who transported the women."

"If that bartender is hanging tough, I have just the energy we need to soften him up."

"Even after finding your woman, you're still bloodthirsty," Dro quipped.

Ryan smirked. "Well see, if you had let me at him, Daron wouldn't have to take the long route to get the information he needs."

"You're beginning to worry me." Dro held on to the handle in the roof as Ryan turned onto another street. "One of the things we try to do in our operations is to leave only minor damage behind, if possible."

"Trust me, I understand that. But in a situation like this, since they weren't thinking about these women, we owe them no courtesies."

"We're going to keep a close eye on you." He let out a hearty chuckle. "You and Shaz both have a calm exterior, but when anyone gets you riled up, there's hell to pay."

"I'm fine now, but know that if we hadn't found Aziza ... "

"I hear that and I understand because, like I told you, I've been in that position."

Only the smooth hum of the engine broke the silence until they stopped outside the warehouse. After a phone call to Daron, the door slid open to admit them.

Bashir sat next to the door keeping guard, while the bartender slumped over the table with his head resting on his folded arms. A few feet away, his partner sat tied to a chair. The fluorescent light illuminated the area where the men were gathered, while the darkness ruled the far corners of the building.

Daron stood next to a shelf, occupied with a gadget in his hand. Two cellular phones and a black box with flashing numbers lay close by.

While Ryan scanned the items, Daron smiled. "Technology is a blessing when you know how to make it work to your advantage."

"I guess those phones belong to these two evil geniuses."

"What they won't tell me, these will." Daron inclined his head toward Jahani's partner in crime. "If he hadn't led us to the lady in red, I'd have finished with this earlier, but all in good time."

Jahani raised his head, then sat up. "This is illegal. You cannot keep me here forever. There will be people looking for me. I have a job and a family."

"Let them look," Ryan snapped. "You should have thought of that before giving drugs to unsuspecting women."

"And who knows how long they've been doing this." Dro squinted over Daron's shoulder.

"Their heydays are coming to an end," Daron said. "We need to establish whether that crooked doctor is connected to them, then we will add these charges on his account."

Jahani's partner glared at them but didn't say another word.

Lowering his voice, Ryan said, "These guys must have a contact inside the police force to get away with these crimes."

Bashir got to his feet and moved closer. "I think you are right. In the past, these offences were like, what do you say ... a slap on the wrist." He nodded sagely. "Since Sheikh Kamran took the throne, things are different in a good way."

"The men who were transporting the women, are they in police custody?" Ryan asked.

"Not quite," Daron said, still focused on his electronic device. "Two of them were shot when everything went down. It's not certain they will survive. There's a third man, one of the security guards. He wasn't shot, but because of the seriousness of this crime, Sheikh Kamran gave permission for him to be transported to an undisclosed location."

"That, I understand."

"Nicco has their cell phones. I need to get to look at those, too," Daron said. "It'll be the easiest way to tie all of this up, if they're involved. We'll head out in a minute."

Ryan massaged the back of his neck. "I can't imagine what those women must be going through. Free this morning and captive again this afternoon."

"Yes, truth is stranger than fiction." Daron reached inside his pants pocket. He answered his cell phone, listened for a moment, then ended the call. "Things are about to get popping. Seems Nicco convinced that security guard to tell what he knows."

"So much for honor among thieves," Dro said.

Ryan's gaze slid back to the two men at the table. "I say thank God. That way the job of cleaning up their mess is easier."

Chapter 22

Aziza's heart brimmed with happiness as her mother's rich contralto filled her ear—even if she was getting grief. They had chatted for half an hour before her mother, Constance, circled back to when she planned to return to the States.

"After Ryan and I have a chance to talk, I'll let you know."

"I would think you'd be on the first plane out of that place."

Aziza pictured her mother; the milk-chocolate skin of her face creased into a fierce frown as she paced the living room in Evanston.

"Remember I have a job here?"

In fact, Aziza didn't know whether she was still employed. Ryan had checked her into his room, and her name might have triggered curiosity, if anyone was checking closely enough. If that was the case, someone from personnel would want to talk to her soon.

"Well," Mom continued, "If I were you, I'd want to see Duraria behind me."

Aziza's gaze strayed to Sunita, whose head was buried one of the books they bought downstairs. "*Durabia*," she said in response to what she swore was stubbornness on her mother's part. She refused to get the name right.

"Ryan's wrapping up some things here. I'll be perfectly safe."

What Mom didn't know was that Ryan hadn't returned to the suite, but had been in touch with her late last night, early this morning, and at midday. She understood the nature of what he was doing in tandem with the Kings. She was comfortable on her own, knowing he was working for the good of the kidnapped women.

She couldn't wait for Ryan to appear. She'd spent the morning falling asleep in snatches and waking up scared out of her mind. When she gave up on resting, she stared at the river that wound past the hotel, then watched television. Now, she had separation anxiety.

Aziza's attention settled on Sunita, who sat on one sofa, tracing the lines of text in another illustrated book.

Her mind came back to the conversation when her mother said, "I need to have a word with Ryan. He has a good head on his shoulders."

"That's why you should trust me when I say we'll be okay. If I didn't love you, I'd be offended that you trust him more than me."

Mom laughed, but only for a few seconds. "No, honey, I don't, but you can't imagine the relief. I don't know if I had a solid night's rest since they took you." Her voice was teary when she continued, "I just want you here, at home, where I can see you."

"I'll ask Drake to set up a video call, so you can see I'm in one piece. Shouldn't you be worried about him?"

"Your brother is as right as rain. They broke up the largest kidney stone with laser surgery. I've been talking to him about his diet for years. This will teach him." She lowered the sound on her television, then said, "Your father wants to speak with you."

"Hey, sugar plum." Martin Hampton cleared his throat, and Aziza knew he was trying to control his emotions. He hadn't called her that in years, but she imagined him hugging her mother while they sat together on the large sofa. The two of them were inseparable, even now. She visualized him, a heavy-set, light-skinned man, his beard sprinkled with gray. Her heart ached because until then, Aziza hadn't realized how much she missed her parents.

"It is so good to hear your voice, but I'm going to echo your mother." Her father's deep voice cut into her musing. "I can't imagine you'd want to continue working in a place where you don't feel safe."

She didn't want to build their hopes that she'd be home in a few days. Many things had been left unspoken between Ryan and her. Although he didn't want to be apart from her, Ryan hadn't definitively laid out a blueprint for how things would look after they left Durabia.

Aziza wasn't sure she even wanted her job back. Taking an assignment in a faraway place had been an adventure when she decided to get away after her last relationship ended. Her father was right. She wasn't sure she'd ever feel safe here again. Plus, there was the fact that Ryan had to return to Paradise Island at some point. Yet, being with Ryan in Durabia changed everything. She let out her breath and admitted, "I do have a few things to sort out before I think about coming home."

"I understand that, sugar. You better tell Ryan that if anything else happens to you, I'm holding him accountable. We're grateful and all, but still … "

After reassuring him she'd be careful, Aziza bade both of them goodbye and called the women's shelter named after Amanda Maharaj that she'd looked up in the directory. After a request routed through two different women, Aziza was able to speak to Naima.

"Hey, I hope you had a good sleep last night and that you're okay."

"We are all thankful. I'm praying the others will return safely." She exhaled on a heavy sigh. "We had a vigil last night."

Aziza's heart sank. While she was resting comfortably in a hotel room, they had been up praying. She had called the center once after Ryan left, but knew it was too late to get anyone on the phone. After a restless night, Aziza still felt tired and her fist was sore. She ignored the discomfort, and holding her breath, she asked, "Is Ahaba with you?"

Naima's silence told the tale.

"Oh, God, no." A boulder sat in her stomach, and she felt even worse about her good fortune.

"We were separated when we walked outside the clinic. She got into the first vehicle … "

"Ryan and the team are still searching," Aziza said quickly. "They won't give up until they find them."

In a soft tone, Naima said, "We are praying they come back."

Aziza sighed and pushed away the heaviness in her spirit. "I have to take care of something now, but I'll call you when I come back. Please tell the other ladies I said hello."

"I will. Stay safe."

"You, too."

Her gaze settled on Sunita, who was still mesmerised by the picture book.

Aziza half rose from the sofa before the phone rang again. Searching her brain as to who could be calling, she lifted the handset then cracked a smile. This was Ryan's room, not hers.

"Good afternoon, may I speak with Miss Aziza Hampton?"

Her heart missed a beat, but she steadied her voice and sat on the edge of the sofa. "Speaking. May I ask who's calling?"

"I am Claudia Gonsalves, from the personnel department of the hotel. We understand that you're checked in as a guest."

Her hackles rose, but Aziza answered in an even tone. "Yes, that's true."

"Can you come to personnel in a half-hour?"

Her promise to Ryan and his words echoed in her head. *Promise me you won't leave this suite until I return.*

"Is there a particular reason you want to meet with me today?" she asked.

"Well, your pay and commission are in jeopardy since you abandoned the job—"

Aziza's blood turned molten, and she clenched her jaw and spoke through her teeth. "I did not *abandon the job* as you put it. For this entire work week, I've been … " She didn't want to talk about yesterday or any of the days before that, so she changed tack. "Never mind, but your accusation is unjustified."

"Well, based on company policy, if someone does not show up after two consecutive days … "

At that point, she stopped listening. She'd given her best to the hotel and deserved every cent she'd worked for in her time there. No way was she about to walk away and let them keep her hard-earned commission.

"So, if you don't show up to the office for this meeting … "

Aziza zoned out again. Ryan expected her to stay put, but she had matters to settle now. She had to at least show up to be able to collect what was due to her. If her luck didn't turn, she'd be back before he returned. "I will be down in a while."

After she replaced the phone, Aziza stood. "Sunita, we have to go out for a short time. Can you change into the sweat bottoms and t-shirt?"

After putting the book aside, Sunita scooted off the sofa.

Aziza went with her to the closet and pulled the items of clothing off the luggage holder. Then she slipped into the Chinese style casual dress she had bought for herself.

The moment she opened the door to the corridor, panic swept over her. The same sensation held her prone to the mattress when she woke at 2:00 a.m. to find that Ryan had not returned. She'd sat up and switched on the light to reassure herself she was not inside the container. Then her thoughts returned to the women who were missing. She said a prayer for them, checked on Sunita, then tried to fall asleep again, but it was dawn before her eyes closed.

Aziza squared her shoulders, gripped Sunita's hand, and made her way to the administrative block, annexed to the main building.

She waited ten minutes to see the human resources director and ensured Sunita remained in the spacious office with them. She was far enough away not to hear the entire conversation. After sitting like a statue for a minute, Sunita turned and stared through the plate-glass at Durabia's capital city below.

The Caucasian woman, who identified herself as the HR director, opened a file Aziza assumed was hers. "My assistant said you claimed you didn't abandon the job."

"I'm sure the hotel reported me as missing to the police. Isn't that the case?"

"Well—"

Aziza sat forward. "So, if you know the reason for my absence, why are you giving me a hard time?"

"The hotel's policy is that—"

"I don't give a rat's behind about your policy," Aziza spat, then glanced toward Sunita. "When I didn't turn up for work after two days, didn't it occur to anyone that something must have happened to me, especially since my things are still in the apartment where I live? That's if you haven't had my possessions thrown out."

The woman had the grace to lower her eyes as her skin flushed. "No, we have removed nothing."

"Did you even check back with the police for an update?"

Valencia Hamilton—according to her name plate—squared her shoulders. "This is not the first time a worker has disappeared—"

"And clearly, none of you cared enough to do anything about it." Waving one hand, Aziza said, "All that matters to this establishment is money."

"I'm sorry you feel that way, but—"

Aziza was in no mood to deal with a trite semi-apology that rang hollow. She looked Ms. Hamilton dead in the eyes. "The woman I was sharing the apartment with, is she still working for the company?"

"Of course, both of you signed your contracts at the same time."

"Since my things are still in there, I need a key to get inside. Mine was stolen."

"I don't think—"

Aziza's patience went AWOL, and she stabbed the desk with one finger. Pain radiated from her still tender knuckles, which made her temper spike. "I didn't resign, and you *know* they took me against my will, the least you can do is let me get my stuff."

Sunita turned from the window to stare at Aziza, who stretched her lips in a tight smile to reassure the child. "It's okay, sweetie. Auntie is fine."

But she wasn't. Nor was she in mental condition to be haggling with anybody. What she needed was peace and the chance to heal from the trauma inflicted on her soul.

Her gaze went back to the dark-haired woman, who leaned forward with both arms on the desk. "I know this may sound strange but here's what I can offer: since you were missing for a week, we can take you back if you reapply for the job. There are strict employment procedures based on your contract—"

Aziza counted to five before she spoke. "Look, I'm not in the mood for any of this after what I've been through. I need a key to that apartment and I'm not leaving here without it."

With her eyes laser focused on Ms. Hamilton, Aziza stared her down in a silent battle of wills, until the HR director picked up her phone and asked someone to bring her a key.

Aziza was well aware that based on Julene's duty roster, she was likely to be at home, but the HR director didn't need to know that fact. They sat in silence, while Aziza glowered at the woman across the desk as she tried to make amends with weak excuses to pacify Aziza. No doubt, she didn't want Aziza to make a stink about the situation.

When a staff member arrived, and Aziza received the key, she got to her feet.

The slender woman frowned. "So what about the job?"

"Don't worry about that because I wouldn't work here, even if you offered me twice my salary. Let me know when my pay for the last two weeks I worked is ready. *Plus, the commission.*"

She stood, and the woman flinched.

Aziza motioned to Sunita, smiling despite the desire to slap someone. "Let's go, sweetie."

As Miss Hamilton kept a wary gaze on her, Aziza said, "You know where to find me."

Chapter 23

The doors of the meat-packing facility slid open, and a container truck rolled out. Arabic lettering stretched along the side, but the graphic of sheep advertised that the refrigerated unit contained meat.

Five miles away, Daron and Dro had their gazes fastened to their phones. Through some technological wizardry invented by Calvin Atwood, a Knight of the Castle, Daron had provided the crew of six with an app that allowed all of them to track the movement of their target. They sat inside a black air-conditioned SUV, running through the details of the rescue.

"We don't want to rack up any casualties," Dro addressed Ryan, wearing a wry grin, "which is why you and I are assigned to break whatever barriers we need to, and get the women to safety."

"You make me sound like a loose cannon, but I'm cool." Ryan tapped his ankle holster and hid a smile. "Now if my woman was still in the wind, you'd have to worry. Aziza is safe, so I'm mellow. The fact that these women are not, means someone is still going to catch these hands."

Chuckles filled the interior of the vehicle.

"We'll all be in a better frame of mind when this is over." Dro said.

"We still have to find those girls," Ryan reminded them. "I won't be at rest until they're all safe."

Their current plan was that Nicco, the designated driver, would intercept the truck from the opposite direction, forcing the crew to stop. If that didn't work, Daron had some wicked diamond-shaped metal canisters that opened into jagged teeth capable of shredding tires.

Under threat of being behind bars for the rest of his life—in a neighboring country, where the facilities were of a much poorer standard— the man they were still holding gave them details of when the women were due to be shipped out of Durabia. According to him, the seven females would cross the border into Nadaum the day after their capture. That was today.

Planning their strategy kept the team up for most of the night and in the early morning, exhaustion forced them to camp on the available beds and man-sized sofas around Daron's suite within Khalil's palatial home. After a few hours of shut-eye, they rose to finalize their plans.

The driver they were holding told them a convoy of trucks was scheduled to leave the meat packing plant at staggered times. The truck carrying the women was leaving at ten a.m., the last of four units in their morning delivery shift.

When Ryan asked how they'd know for certain which vehicle the women were stowed in, Daron had shared the extent of his and Calvin's brilliance. Among his digital tools was a scanner that could perform something akin to an X-ray function from as far away as a quarter of a mile. Ryan was impressed and optimistic that they would complete the task assigned to them by Sheikh Kamran, whom he'd met last night. Their assignment from him was to rescue the women at any cost.

As the trucks rolled out, Daron focused on his phone. "Time to get rolling," he said. "I'm scanning all the units in case there's been a change of plan."

Nicco faced forward and got them moving. They cruised along the asphalt, getting themselves into position. The truck was headed from the outskirts of Hanan along an isolated stretch of road that led into the desert. Their destination was ten miles away, just over the border in Nadaum. When the behemoth of a vehicle crept over the horizon, Nicco cruised along, timing the approach of the laden haulage unit.

The air inside the SUV was tense as they waited for him to be close enough to make his move. When he came within a hundred yards of the truck, Nicco spun the SUV into its path, then back to his side of the road, giving the impression that he was either drunk or ill.

The speed of the oncoming vehicle didn't vary.

Nicco repeated his maneuver, while Ryan squinted hard at the oncoming vehicle. By this time, the cab of the eighteen wheeler was visible. The driver leaned over the steering wheel, staring through the windscreen, clearly concerned.

"I don't have enough room to do that again without getting us all killed," Nicco said in a matter-of-fact tone, despite the urgency of their situation. "We'll need those wheel shredders."

"Say no more." Daron leaned out the window and with a backhanded swing, tossed a handful of the metallic items that burst open on contact with the asphalt.

The truck was now upon them with nowhere to go except over the shredders.

A mixture of curiosity and fright filled the eyes of the driver. The wheels made loud popping sounds as they rolled over the metal shards.

Daron directed another handful under the body of the container as it passed them. The muted explosions continued as Nicco slammed the brake and they all jumped out of the SUV.

Daron and Dro approached the doors with guns drawn.

"Get out with your hands up," Dro yelled. "Both of you."

For a moment there was no movement, then the door opened.

Dro stepped back as the driver stumbled out of his seat. The man on the passenger side jumped down and stuck his hands in the air.

"We have only meat," the driver said, his gaze darting toward Bashir, Nicco, Ryan, and Angela, who surrounded them.

"I'll be the judge of that," Dro said, with one hand outstretched. The 9mm Sig Sauer in his other hand didn't waver. "Give me the keys to the back."

"I cannot do that." The short man sweated profusely under the blinding sunlight.

Daron herded the passenger closer to the driver, while Dro cocked his gun. "Either you let us into the truck or I give you a taste of what this baby can do. Trust me, you won't like it."

With shaking hands, the driver handed him the key ring. "Those will not help you. We do not have the keys or the combination. When we get to the destination, the people there open the freezer and remove the meat."

The young man bobbed his head as if the frantic motions would save his life. In deeply accented English, he said, "We cannot get inside. It is the company policy."

Daron and Dro exchanged a glance. "All these precautions for something as simple as food tells me there's more here than can be seen with the naked eye," Daron said with a smirk.

Nicco and Angela went into a huddle near the SUV. Daron joined them seconds later, leaving Bashir, Dro, and Ryan to deal with the men from the truck.

Dro directed them to the side of the road with his gun.

"You are going to get us fired," the driver yelled. "This unit is refrigerated, and we need to go before everything is rotten."

"You left the engine running, so it's all good," Ryan said dryly. "We'll try not to keep you long."

Bashir pursed his lips while his eyes twinkled.

Daron, Nicco, and Angela left the SUV and approached the back of the truck, where Daron attached an oblong silver object near the electronic lock. When it started beeping, he waved them back with one hand. "This won't affect the cooler operations, but it's loud. Cover your ears," he warned Bashir and Ryan.

With a bang, the doors flew open.

Dro and Ryan climbed into the back. Pallets loaded with white boxes lined both sides of the forty-foot container. When they had gone halfway down the length of the body, Dro and Ryan exchanged a look. Although there was nothing to prove the women were inside, adrenaline rushed through Ryan's body. He tapped one container. Though it felt solid under his hand, he had the uncomfortable thought that some of these foam boxes might be transporting body parts encased in ice. He turned his mind away from that scenario. He had learned that positive thoughts encouraged him and assisted with good outcomes.

They were now deep inside the container and stood in a wide space between the boxes and the cab, which made little sense to either of them. The same curiosity he felt was reflected in Dro's eyes. Ryan tapped on what seemed to be a solid wall, then laid the palm of his hand on the metal. It was freezing cold.

He angled his head closer, certain he heard movement. He rapped harder on the surface. The noise from the other side increased, as if someone was letting him know they were inside. Ryan and he shared a knowing look, then turned their attention to the sheet of metal. They searched for the lever that would give them access to the hidden compartment.

"Can you hear me?" Ryan asked, raising his voice

A titter of excitement rose beyond the wall, plus a jumble of indistinct words that neither he nor Dro could decipher.

"I think that's a yes," Dro answered as a grin lit his eyes. "*And* I believe I've found the hinge."

The panel slid toward them, and they moved out of the way. The door opened to reveal a group of women all standing side by side along the walls of the narrow metal box, wearing the hospital gowns they had been given the day before. The compartment had been built so that they couldn't sit or move close together. Fear clouded their eyes as they shivered, their hands confined in front of them with handcuffs.

The blast of frigid air angered Ryan, who wanted to have a face to face with whoever locked them inside without adequate protection from the cold. Then a darker thought hit him. These women were in a refrigerated truck, with barely any clothing, and at a temperature level that would kill them. This set-up would preserve their organs until they made it to their destination.

"We're not here to hurt you," Ryan said in a soothing tone.

"That is what those two drivers said before they were killed and those other men lumped us into another van," a Black woman with a

British accent said indignantly. She glared at Dro and Ryan, as if she was the protector of the group.

"We understand and respect your feelings." Dro held up both hands. "As we speak, the police, the Sheikh, his wife, and other officials are on their way."

"And if you don't feel you can trust them," Ryan added, "the media is aware of your situation. That puts a spotlight on what has happened to all of you."

Their Kings' plan to expose the kidnappings was intended to put the perpetrators at a disadvantage. The trafficking of women and harvesting their organs were too important to pretend they weren't happening. The Kings', as experts brought in to clean up the crimes, would have to share their findings. In support, the Sheikh had scheduled a press briefing to take place immediately after they finished the operation. They all agreed that once they found the women, it would be time to lean harder on those doing the dirty work for the people at the top of the chain of operation.

The women shuffled their bare feet and whispered to each other, as if unsure they could trust the two men.

"I'll be back in a second," Dro said as he walked away.

Ryan held his position outside the doorway, sickened by the fact that the women preferred to stay in the cold, rather than trust another man—even if he didn't look like the ones who kidnapped them. When the phone vibrated against his leg, he put a hand over it and slid it out of his pocket. Only Aziza could be calling him at this time. He'd told her the operation could take anywhere from two to three hours, but she insisted that she needed to know the minute they found the women.

After he explained that the extraction might mean hand-to-hand combat and an intensive clean-up operation, Aziza insisted that he talk to her as soon as was humanly possible. She hadn't given an inch. Her face flashed across the screen, and he smiled. This time, her stubbornness was helpful. He now had a way to convince the women that Dro and he were legit.

"Did you find them?" Aziza asked.

What about a hello, he wanted to ask, but this wasn't the time for jokes. "D'you mind if I put you on speaker, Aziza?"

"Why?"

"We just found the women, but after what happened they're not about to trust us."

"Of course," she said.

He tapped the button, then Aziza said, "Ahaba, are you there?"

A teenager stepped forward, her eyes filled with relief. "Aziza, is that you?"

"Yes, it's me. Hey, everybody."

They greeted her in a chorus, then went silent with their gazes glued to the cellular.

"I know you have no reason to trust anybody, but these are good men. They will help you. Just like they helped me."

The females exchanged wary glances, but Ryan understood their reaction.

After studying him for a moment, the slender girl in front of him said, "Okay, we will trust these two."

"Thank you," he said to Aziza.

"I'm so glad you found them. It would have been hard getting past this tragedy if those men had succeeded with this crime. "

The nearby wail of a police siren and Dro's hand on his shoulder, told him it was time to get the women out of the container.

"Where did they keep you last night?" he asked.

"In di back of di meat factory, in a nasty, stinkin' room," a woman with a Jamaican accent answered.

"I'm sorry to hear that. Thank you," he said as he turned aside. "Zee, I gotta go. I'll see you when we finish here."

"I'll be waiting. I love you, Ryan."

For no reason he could name, his throat clogged. Then he swallowed and put a smile in his voice. "I love you, too, Zee."

Dro gave him an approving nod and headed back the way he'd come.

After slipping the phone back into his pocket, Ryan led the group through the acre of boxes. When they made it to the door of the unit,

Angela was waiting with a stack of blankets. Each woman wrapped herself in the thick fabric.

Again, Ryan wondered what kind of men would shut women inside a refrigerated container without giving them a means to stay warm. But, if they considered them merchandise, they wouldn't care what became of them as long as they reached the buyers alive.

Amanda Maharaj arranged for a mobile medical unit on location. While a doctor examined the women, the police fielded questions from the media, who descended on the scene.

The two policemen they met early in the week didn't seem to know what to do with themselves. The assistant commissioner looked at his watch, as if he had important business to conduct elsewhere, while the commissioner did his best to avoid looking at the container or the women.

By that time, the police had already taken the driver and his assistant into custody for questioning. Among the team, they decided Bashir and Ryan would travel with the women and field questions from them. Daron, Dro, Nicco, and Angela left with the police in a speeding convoy headed to the meat packing plant. When they completed that part of the operation, the plan was to have another go at the man they were holding at the warehouse before releasing him to the police. The Sheikh had promised them immunity over the kidnappings during their assignment.

Ryan knew it would be some time before he saw Aziza, but the fact that she was safe made all the difference. He hoped the rest of the operation and the debriefing wouldn't consume the entire day because he couldn't let another one pass before having a serious discussion with Aziza.

Their future depended on it.

Chapter 24

Julene's face went slack when Aziza greeted her. When she could speak, she pulled Aziza into a hug. "OMG! I am so happy to see you." She stepped away but held on to her with both hands. "I thought Deirdre said you weren't coming back. I prayed so many times that you—"

Aziza bypassed Julene's obvious joy with a question. "Why was she so sure I wouldn't return?"

Julene pressed both hands to her eyes. "It's just that she was with you that night and because this has happened to others, she figured you wouldn't turn up alive."

"Well, here I am. Can I come inside?"

Aziza only asked because Julene had met her at the door when it opened.

"Of course." Julene backed away and moved into their living room.

As always, whenever she was off work, Julene dressed in sweat bottoms and a tank top. Her caramel complexion and abundance of loose curls gave people the impression that she was related to Aziza. The major difference between them was that Aziza stood almost a foot taller. They had gotten along since the moment they met. At the time, nearly a year ago, the hotel placed them together in the fully-furnished housing units they provided for workers at lower than commercial rental rates.

Aziza guided Sunita inside. "I have company."

Showing her a dimpled smile, Julene waved one hand. "Sure, I don't mind."

Julene plopped down on the oversized brown sofa. "What happened to you?" she asked, "And who's this little angel?"

Aziza wasn't sure how to answer and didn't want to have to extract herself from an uncomfortable conversation. She sat, and Sunita did the same. "I'm just watching her for a few days," she said while her gaze wandered around the living area. Only a week had passed and yet the cozy apartment felt foreign despite the familiar furnishings, like the huge metal clock that graced one wall. She'd bought it in a souk just outside of the city because of the unusual design.

"So are you coming back to work?" Julene asked, totally focused on Aziza.

"I doubt it," Aziza said. "After the experience I've had, I don't know how long I'll be here."

"So, were you really kidnapped? That's what I heard around the hotel, but knowing you, I wondered if it was true. We all know you can take care of yourself." She paused for a few seconds then added, "It's so ironic that you hardly ever go out and then when you did, you ended up missing."

"I'm giving God thanks because this could have ended differently." The enormity of being sold as a sex slave or killed for her organs swept over Aziza and silenced her for a moment. "Were it not for Ryan's cousin, plus the strings he pulled, I might have ended up dead."

Leaning forward, Julene said, "Although people talk about women of our kind disappearing, I've not been in contact with anyone who has been unlucky like that." She pulled at one of her curls as she continued, "The hotel questioned all of us, but aside from reporting you missing to the police, I don't know if they did more than that, and aside from one interview on Tuesday, the police have not spoken with me again. Did they even inform your family?"

"They didn't have to do that. I'm usually in contact with my mother and when she didn't hear from me on her birthday last Saturday, she started calling my phone."

A cool breeze wafted through the window and teased Aziza's skin. Such a tiny observation, but it made her glad to be alive.

"So, if you end up not staying, they'll pair me up with another roommate." Julene sounded despondent.

"I'll tell you for sure what I'm doing in another couple of days," Aziza said, although she knew this chapter of her life was closed. The news would filter down from personnel, eventually. Julene loved to talk, so staying quiet about her decision gave Aziza some level of privacy.

"For now, I'll just grab some of my things. I'm staying at the hotel with Ryan, so you know where to reach me."

She squeezed Sunita's shoulder and they stood. The first thing Aziza did when they entered the bedroom was to open the drapes to let in more light. The street below was busy, as always, but the view was beautiful. Hanan was still a wonderful place, despite her misfortune. She packed a small bag and gathered her toiletries, plus her digital camera. The pictures held memories of her time in the country before disaster hit her. Everything else she needed rested with Ryan.

She had now been out of the suite for close to two hours, and a pang of anxiety squeezed her stomach and cast a shadow over her mood. Her gaze went to Sunita, who stood with both hands pressed to the glass. She was such a well-behaved child. Too well behaved. In her limited English, she had told Aziza she was happy to escape from *El Zalaam*.

Aziza listened in horror while Sunita shared that she was from neighboring Nadaum, and her father had sent her to the *El Zalaam* because their family had ten children and needed the money. She spent a year in *El Zalaam*, and though she was stoic as she told her story, Aziza knew the child would need therapy. No one walked away unscathed from being a sexual plaything. Not even a child this young.

With a light pitch to her voice, she said, "Let's go, Sunita."

The girl turned from the window and stood by the bed, gazing at the row of teddy bears lined up in front of the pillows. The longing in her eyes caught Aziza unawares. She took so much for granted, and Sunita's wonder with every new experience made it obvious she'd never had much.

"Would you like one?" Aziza asked.

Sunita's eyes shone when she looked at Aziza. "Yes, please."

"Choose the one you like most," Aziza said.

Sunita leaned against the mattress and picked up a fat brown and cream bear. She held it up. "This one."

Picking up her bag, Aziza said, "Take another one."

The child's mouth opened, then she smiled. Her pure joy made Aziza eyes smart while her heart hurt. A soft pink and white bear went under Sanita's other arm. Her teeth gleamed in a delighted grin.

"Let's go back to our room."

With her new toys pressed to her chest, Sunita nodded.

In the living room, Aziza and Julene exchanged another hug. Then Aziza and her small companion left for the hotel, which lay a few streets away. The walk was what Aziza needed to clear her head. Being in her old surroundings was a good thing. Now, more than ever, she was sure of what she wanted.

Her footsteps quickened the closer she came to the hotel. She rushed into the elevator and took Sunita's hand as they walked down the corridor on their floor. Aziza sucked in a deep breath when they entered the suite, then switched on the television and scrolled to Discovery Kids. "You can watch cartoons for five minutes. Then we'll grab something to eat, okay?"

Sunita gently laid the stuffed toys on the sofa bed. "Lunch."

Aziza grinned. "Good girl. Yes, we'll have lunch."

She unpacked the bag, then dialed Ryan's number. After their tense ten-minute call, she sent up a prayer of thanks that the missing women and Ryan were safe. Only the girls now remained to be found. Ryan had reassured her the other men were still chasing clues to discover their whereabouts.

She felt like celebrating this victory, and after washing her hands and face, she supervised Sunita in cleaning hers. Then she retrieved the camera from her bag with a wry smile, thinking how addicted she was to technology. For now, she didn't have a phone but the camera might come in useful. A moment later, they headed downstairs to one of the cafes.

They sat at a table next to a wall of glass, which gave them a view of a golden urn spewing water. She ordered a hamburger and fries, which she shared with Sunita. Aziza had learned that everything was super-sized in Durabia.

The café was nearly empty and after Aziza glanced around them, she pointed to Sunita's plate. "Do you remember what that is called?"

Holding a fry next to her lips, Sunita nodded. "Hamburger."

"And what are you holding in your hand?"

"Frenchy fry?"

Aziza held back a grin. "French fry."

With the utmost care, Sunita repeated her words then bit into the sliver of potato.

Her lips were wrapped around the burger bun when a familiar figure strode down the corridor directly in front of the restaurant. Aziza couldn't miss Akbar. He had sleek, black hair that he styled and kept in place with mousse, but the feature that set him apart was the tiny stud he wore in one ear. The hotel held the staff to the strictest standards, but somehow he got away with wearing that diamond earring. His black, long-sleeve shirt let her know he was either on duty, or would be soon.

A tall, distinguished man in a suit walked next to him. The two were deep in conversation.

Going on instinct, Aziza snapped a picture of the two of them. She didn't know how she was going to broach the subject of seeing him with Ryan, but she'd figure that out when the time came.

"What is that, Auntie?"

"I'm taking pictures. It's a camera," Aziza said as her gaze swung back to Akbar.

As if he sensed someone watching him, Akbar's gaze swept the immediate area around him. Then the man with him spoke and they stepped into a cigar store.

Her first reaction was to confront him, but Ryan's warning held her back. Plus a flash of memory—an image of herself taking unsteady steps to the ladies' room. His offer to help. Her refusal. Then another man appearing. Although they didn't speak, she could have sworn they communicated with their eyes. That other man insisted on helping her down the corridor. From there, a blank space developed in her memory. Her next conscious thought came after waking up in that container feeling as if she'd been through a wringer.

She wasn't certain Akbar had anything to do with selling her out, but her instincts killed her doubts. She distinctly remembered he was friendly with the men behind the bar and her drink was the only way they could have introduced drugs into her system. Proving he was involved in drugging and kidnapping her would be hard. Plus, there was the business of telling Ryan that she'd seen Akbar. He wouldn't be happy about her being anywhere downstairs. Despite that, she had business to do and was relatively safe in the hotel and its surroundings. *But Encounters should also have been safe.*

When she faced forward, Sunita was watching her. "Are you okay?"

She had asked Sunita that question so many times in the last twenty-four hours, the child was now using that phrase back to her. Aziza smiled widely and patted her hand. "I'm fine, baby girl."

But her appetite had left. She now felt threatened, but didn't want to alarm Sunita. With a smile in place, she said, "Let's go back to our room."

They were halfway through the door when Akbar emerged from the shop and stood talking with the same companion.

Sunita tugged on her hand, but Aziza didn't respond.

Their eyes met, and Akbar's face twisted. His expression ran the gamut from consternation to horror. Instead of greeting her, he quickened his steps. "Aziza."

At her side, Sunita pointed toward the man with Akbar. In a shaky voice, she cried, "I know him."

Chapter 25

Ryan closed his laptop and got up from the desk. He'd expected to find Aziza in the room, but she had disappeared. A look around the bathroom and in the closet told him she'd left under her own steam. Several items were moved out of place, the way she tended to do when she was going out. The question was why she left after promising she'd stay in the suite.

He had finished a brief telephone call with Myles and agreed to a virtual meeting in a few days to include their client in Jamaica. At that time, they would finalize several clauses in the draft contract.

Aziza still hadn't returned, and he was sliding from anxiety into anger. She had to know he'd be worried if she disappeared for any length of time. Worse, she hadn't left a note.

He sat on the side of the bed with his head cupped in his hands, fighting to stay alert. The lack of sleep made him drift in and out of consciousness, but he knew the moment Aziza arrived back at the suite. He felt her aura, but something was amiss. He sat up, then stood, poised to deal with whoever had dared to frighten her.

"Hurry! Go into the bedroom and close the door," she yelled.

What the hell?

He stalked to the closet, opened the safe he'd secured only moments ago, and stepped back into the bedroom.

Sunita barrelled into the suite with tears streaking her cheeks. At the sight of him, she opened her mouth wide, as if to scream, but he put a finger to his lips and pointed to the closet. She followed his direction and dragged it shut.

He rushed toward the door at the same moment Aziza ran inside and tried to shut it. Ryan pulled her out of the way and let the person behind her stumble inside. He grabbed the man by the material of his shirt and pressed the gun to his forehead. "You better have a good explanation for why you're in my suite and why you're chasing this woman."

The man sputtered, then spoke in a wheedling tone. "I wanted to talk to her."

Aziza darted out from behind Ryan. "You only wanted to speak to me, but you chased us and scared us half to death?"

He grimaced and twisted his body to escape Ryan's grasp. "If you do not mind, I will leave now."

Ryan cocked the gun. "That's not how this works."

"I am—"

"Say a word or move a muscle *if* you want to meet your maker."

Akbar lapsed into silence as both the pupils and the whites of his eyes expanded.

Without looking at Aziza, Ryan said, "My phone is on the bedside table. Get Dro on the line and tell him to come right now."

She did as he asked while he backed Akbar into the living area.

Ryan pushed him into one of the chairs at the dining table, pulled out another, and faced him. "You're going to tell me what business you have with my woman, so think carefully about what you plan to tell me."

"He's on the way," Aziza said, stepping out of the bedroom.

"Thanks. Is Sunita all right?" Ryan's attention did not stray from the man in front of him.

"She will be, no thanks to him."

Akbar jerked back and looked at his watch.

"Need to be somewhere?" Ryan asked.

Arms folded, Akbar said, "I am on duty in another hour."

Ryan's attention shifted to the logo on his black shirt. "You should have thought of that earlier."

A knock came at the door, and Aziza went to answer.

Dro greeted her and walked to Ryan's side. "You're coming with us," he said.

"Where are we going?" Akbar asked, breathing hard. "You cannot do this. I am a citizen of Durabia. I have to be at work."

"Don't worry about it," Dro said, "You'll find out shortly. And your citizenship has nothing to do with this matter."

"But—"

"Resisting won't help you." Ryan handed his gun to Dro, then guided Aziza to the bedroom. Over his shoulder, he said, "I'll only be a minute."

When they stood just inside the bedroom door, Ryan glanced at Sunita who sat cross-legged on the mattress supporting her cheeks with her fists. He pulled Aziza into a quick hug and murmured in her ear. "I'll be away for at least a few more hours with what's his name ... Akbar."

She pulled away to ask, "How did you know?"

"He's one of the first persons I investigated when I arrived here."

"Good. For all we know, he's done this to other women. Where are you taking him?"

Aziza met his steady gaze, then sighed. "I get it. You can't tell me. Just come back safely."

"I will." He kissed her forehead. "For heaven's sake, don't go anywhere. And by the way, that discussion isn't finished. Well, we didn't have a chance to get started."

"I won't leave." She had the grace to look contrite. "Trust me."

Ryan cocked one brow, and she smiled. "I really am sorry. I should have listened to you."

"Yes, you should have."

He approached the bed and sat a few inches from Sunita, who had salt lines marking the path of her tears. She looked up at him, eyes still wet and her lips pulled down at the corners.

"I'm sorry about everything, but it will be okay. Aziza and I will take care of you."

"The man with him." She jabbed her finger at the living area. "I saw him at *El Zalaam*. He has girls like me."

"Let me show you." Aziza left the room and returned with a digital camera, explaining. "I threw it behind the couch when I came in."

She brought up the picture she'd taken and told him of the men's movements.

"Mind if I take this?" he asked.

"Of course not, and please ensure you get those girls back. I haven't forgotten."

Ryan chuckled and touched her cheek. "Aziza, I love you, I really do, but sometimes I think you'll be the death of me."

"I'll be praying while you're gone, but you're tough." She patted his cheek, wearing a somber expression. "You'll survive."

He pressed a kiss to her temple and strode into the living room, where Dro and Akbar stood by the door.

Before they stepped out of the suite, Dro pointed to Akbar. "I explained to our friend here that Sheikh Kamran is part of this operation, in case he decides to make a break for it."

"I told you I do not know anything of this *operation*," Akbar spat through his teeth.

"That's fine," Ryan said, "because nobody asked you anything. Yet."

They took the elevator, swept through the lobby, and declined the valet service. Standing around out front would only give Akbar an opportunity to elude them, if he got the chance.

Dro sat in the back of the black Ford F 150 pickup truck they exchanged with the Limo after the rescue yesterday. Akbar stared outside the entire time on the half-hour journey to the warehouse where Vikkas, Daron, and Bashir waited, after being called en route. Nicco, Hassan, and Rahm would join them if they needed more manpower for what would be their next assignment.

On arrival, they hustled Akbar into the warehouse and gave him a seat.

Ryan brought up the picture Aziza took and sat adjacent to Akbar. "This man, who is he?"

After gazing at the camera with a blank expression, Abkar said, "I do not know him well."

"That's not what I asked. Try again."

The men stood around the metal table waiting for his response. When he didn't speak, Vikkas planted both hands on the surface. "Let me explain something to you, in case you don't understand what's happening. You're in deep trouble for the part you've played in abducting and selling women. It was only a matter of time before we came for you. We will think about not sending you to prison forever *if* you save us the trouble of having to hunt this man down."

Akbar studied his hands, then said, "His name is Madhav Hadad."

Daron picked up a tablet, inputted some information, and turned it to face Vikkas, who winced. His focus turned to Akbar. "What do you and this government official have in common?"

When he didn't answer, Vikkas continued, "Let me guess. Some of the women you've been preying on have passed through his hands."

Akbar frowned and jammed his fingers through his hair. "I did not say that."

"That's fine. You don't have to say anything."

"What about that break you promised me?" Akbar asked, laying both hands in front of him.

"Consider it withdrawn," Vikkas said, barely moving his facial muscles, but the fury flowing off him was unmistakable. "I've reconsidered."

"That little girl," he said with a desperate edge to his voice. "From the container."

"What about her?" Ryan glared at Akbar.

"I can tell you where the other girls are now. The man who collected them works for Hadad."

"And how would you know all of these details?" Vikkas said.

"I was with him when he was making the arrangements to transport them."

His words struck Ryan hard. He still didn't understand how men bought and sold women and children like cattle when they had lives and families.

Staring into Aziza's pain-filled eyes although she was miles away, Ryan said, "Where are the children?"

"Inside *El Zalaam.*"

Dro moved behind Akbar and slapped a pair of handcuffs on him. "Your story had better be true. Otherwise, we will have more problems."

Akbar wriggled in the seat and protested. "But I helped you."

"And we thank you for that." Vikkas smiled as he walked to the door. "But you're still going to jail."

"This is not right, you said—"

"Yeah, yeah," Dro said on his way to the entrance. "*He* considered helping you out, but *I* made no such promise."

Chapter 26

After an impromptu consultation with Sheikh Kamran at his conference center, he signed a decree that gave them permission to raid *El Zalaam.*

He looked up from the document and let his gaze skim the men and the sole woman at the multimedia table. "I believe if we are doing a job, it should be done properly. That means every female must also be removed from *El Zalaam.*"

Hassan and Bashir wore identical expressions—brows raised and mouths slightly open.

"Yes. The time is now," Sheikh Kamran said. "My wife and I have been waiting for the ideal time to address that situation."

The Sheikh ran one hand down the front of his gold tunic. "The Nationals and Durabia Tribunal would not hear of it. They swore only women were brought in."

A ripple of disapproval rose in the room, but the Sheikh raised one hand, and continued speaking. "I warned them, but they didn't listen. Owning these women and children is not illegal at this point, but we will be closing *El Zalaam.*"

"Why not pass it into law, Uncle?" Hassan asked.

The Sheikh scanned the faces of the men at the table. "That is exactly what will happen. At the next tribunal gathering, I will make it clear that we cannot operate as a modern metropolis and have this ugly underbelly that would be considered an atrocity by human rights activists."

Hassan nodded. "That part of our image does need a makeover."

"What does this mean for men like Madhav Hadad, who are in government but practice this kind of evil?" Ryan asked. "Surely kidnapping is a crime."

Sheikh Kamran inclined his head toward Ryan. "Indeed it is, and as long as we have proof ... "

Tapping the glossy surface of the table, Daron said, "If there's any to be found, we'll find it."

"Thank you."

"I have another question," Ryan said. "Won't it be extraordinary to have this decree signed and acted on immediately?"

A steely glint lit the Sheikh's eyes. "It is the prerogative of the Sheikh to act on any urgent matters in the way he sees fit. I will notify the police, so they can provide a security presence, but they won't interfere. They will meet you outside *El Zalaam*.

"My wife and I will put transportation and housing arrangements in place. We will have everything ready and provide support staff by the time you're finished at *El Zalaam*. This meeting is at an end. Let me know the minute your mission is complete."

The group of eight Kings, Knights, plus Nicco and Angela filed out of the multi-story building and gathered around the F 150 truck and a midnight black metallic Toyota Land Cruiser. Rahm and Ryan had been introduced earlier, but didn't have the opportunity to exchange more than a few words. The tattoo artist didn't speak much, but had a commanding presence. After a five-minute conversation, the team organized themselves into two parties and drove to the far end of Hanan.

El Zalaam was a tiny city of its own, behind high walls and an ornate metal gate that ensured the privacy of those who took their pleasure within its confines.

When they arrived at the gate, Hassan got out as the two halves slid open on silent hinges. He opened the parchment document that carried

Sheikh Kamran's seal. The man in front of him stepped back, included a guard in the conversation in a rapid exchange of Arabic, then hurried into the building.

Hassan returned to the window. "He has gone to fetch the woman in charge."

"Technically, we don't need to wait for anyone," Vikkas said. "Not even the police."

As Ryan stepped out of the truck, a marked vehicle pulled up behind them, while ahead of them the gate attendant returned with a middle-aged female wearing a European-style dress. "Why are you here?" she asked, her eyes flashing with irritation. "We have the protection of the Sheikh."

"Not anymore," Vikkas said. "We have an order, which will be enforced."

She refused to step aside. "Let me call—"

"No." Vikkas' tone was more forceful. He looked over his shoulder. "Angela."

She came forward. "You and I are going to your office, room, or whatever space you occupy on these premises."

The woman narrowed her eyes, thought better of defying Angela, and left with her.

"As agreed," Vikkas said, scanning the group, "we're going to do what we have to do."

They moved toward the building as a unit. Closed doors lined a long corridor and branched into another passage. All of them spread out, took a section of each aisle and banged on the doors. As they opened, the men walked inside and scanned the rooms.

Eastern music pervaded the air and in several instances, teenagers clad in sheer material danced in front of men old enough to be their fathers and grandfathers.

Ryan's gaze swept over the well-kept salons, equipped with a sizeable bed and several sofas.

For men to play out their fantasies, some of them perverted.

He pounded on one door, which an annoyed, bare-chested man

yanked open. His demeanor changed when he spotted the gun Ryan held against his thigh. As fright replaced annoyance in his dark eyes, Ryan ignored him and spoke to the tiny girl of African descent, who crouched on one side of the mattress.

Ryan looked her in the eyes, ignoring her hands covering her chest. He pointed to her blouse. "Put on your clothes."

The pain and relief in her eyes revealed how much of her childhood had been stolen at this tender stage of life.

The man found his voice and cursed Ryan, who quieted him with a hard stare.

Ryan's attention cut back to the girl, who now stood next to the bed. With his thumb he pointed over his shoulder, then followed her to the door. Young women of various nationalities stood outside several rooms. From the back of the building Angela approached, carrying an accordion file, while the woman who ruled the place trailed her and waved both hands as if offering an explanation. Angela went past him, throwing words at the other woman, then stopped at the entrance where she spoke to the girls in soft Arabic. Positioned as she was to secure the children, Ryan felt more at ease.

The police did not attempt to interrupt their search, but observed their activities from the courtyard.

They directed all the females to get dressed and stand in the walkway. After scouring the sprawling two-story building, Angela counted thirty girls, half of whom hadn't reached puberty, and five little ones.

The combination of hope and despair in their eyes squeezed Ryan's heart, and he had to look away to relieve the fury gnawing at his stomach. He hated to think that other children might be in this same situation elsewhere in Durabia. Standing tall, he reminded himself they were doing all they could to resolve this situation. Time and opportunity would take care of any other youngsters who needed their help, given the Sheikh's decree.

At the end of the search, they gathered in the courtyard, while the children retrieved the few things they owned under the supervision of the woman in charge.

"Do you know if the four girls taken from the container Aziza was in are among this group?"

Angela held up the file she carried. "Yes, I asked about them specifically. For a ... whatever this place is, they keep good records."

"Well, if the owners are running a business, I'd expect so." Nicco grimaced and let out a deep breath.

"A business built on the suffering of young women." Ryan shook his head. "People kill me, but according to the Bible, the love of money is the root of all kinds of evil."

The bus arrived, and the youngsters filed inside with Angela and Nicco assigned to ride with them to Jai's clinic. After a telephone conversation with the Sheikh, Hassan confirmed that a member of his family, Blair, a surgical nurse at the hospital, would assist with processing the children. Her aunt, the Sheikha, had arranged housing as the Sheikh promised.

Caution kept the team onsite after they escorted the Toyota Coaster bus to the medical facility. Once the children were examined, the F 150 and the Land Cruiser sandwiched the bus to ensure all the passengers arrived safely at the shelter.

Forty-five minutes later, the group separated, with Dro, Ryan, Bashir, and Rahm heading back to the center of Hanan. They left Bashir at his apartment building and arrived at the hotel a few minutes later. While discussing the day's events, they boarded the elevator.

Standing outside the lift on his floor, Dro held the door. "Enjoy the evening. The way things are hopping around here, it wouldn't surprise me if we have to leave again in the middle of the night."

Ryan chuckled, rubbing the back of his neck. "That's if Aziza can wake me. I'm dead on my feet."

"It goes with the territory."

"And we still have outstanding matters to clear up."

Dro released the door. "Yeah, like the scum at the warehouse and the bartender's friend, among other things."

"I forgot about him."

Ryan frowned and stuck his foot in the opening as Dro released dry laughter, then said, "I wouldn't worry about them. They're only getting a taste of the mental anguish those women went through. They'll be fine."

The doors of the elevator closed, and Ryan's mind settled on Aziza. His heart pumped harder, and he smiled in anticipation at the thought of seeing her. If this was how coming home to her felt, he was all in. The exhaustion fell away, and his steps were light on his approach to the suite. Despite his gratefulness, they still had to discuss why she broke his trust.

He was serious about people honoring their word. Life was simpler when one's actions lined up with what was said. His parents' marriage had dissolved because of his mother's inability to believe in his father after he made the mistake of being unfaithful twice—with the same woman. His father eventually got his act straight, re-married, and was able to stay that way.

In a frank conversation, Emory Bostwick admitted to Ryan, "Son, losing your mother is the biggest regret I have and disrespecting her was the stupidest mistake I ever made. Don't let that be your lot in life. It was only after I lost Joyce that I realized she was my soul mate."

Their relationship changed Ryan's mother. She was less open and more watchful. After the divorce, her first visit to Paradise Island had been for a vacation, and she chose the place because of the name. After the hell she had gone through in her marriage, she decided Paradise Island sounded heavenly.

During a week on the island—separated from New Providence by two bridges across the Nassau Harbor—Joyce spent her mornings strolling the white sand beaches while the boys looked for seashells. In the afternoons, she gave them plenty of time to explore the extensive water park and the wide array of rides, some of which brought their hearts into their throats while they yelled with glee.

Months after they returned to Jamaica, she discussed the possibility of moving to the Bahamas and told them she had a job waiting. Myles and Ryan talked about the idea, and chose to stay with her, while their father migrated to Evanston.

Ryan was ten at the time, and Joyce stayed in the Bahamas and eventually become a naturalized citizen. Her partner was a Bahamian man, and though their relationship was still in the present tense, she refused to marry again.

Ryan learned some hard lessons from his parents' breakup and avoided making those mistakes. One relationship at a time was how he'd handled his life up to now, and Aziza was enough woman for him. His mother first met her when they visited for dinner during Aziza's vacation.

While Aziza had gone to the bathroom later in the evening and her beau was at the other end of the verandah smoking a cigar, Joyce asked, "Son, is she the one?"

He thought for only a second, before nodding. "Yes, I believe she is."

Joyce gripped his arm and stared into his eyes. "Love her hard and do whatever it takes to keep her happy. Although I'm over your father's shenanigans, I want to remind you that if you love someone, you protect them with everything in you and you *don't* disrespect your queen and the mother of your children."

The remembered pain that shadowed her eyes touched him deep inside and a memory pulled him into the past. After she threw his father out, he'd walked into their bedroom one night to find her sobbing with her face pressed into the pillow. At the time he didn't know what to do, other than to climb into the bed with her and hug her until he fell asleep. They never spoke about that incident, but Ryan knew in his soul, he never wanted to hurt any woman the way his father had hurt his mother.

As Aziza appeared in the doorway, he held out his hand to her. To his mother, he said, "You didn't have to say a word, Mama. I remember … and I don't want that kind of energy in my home."

She flipped her locs over her shoulders and picked up her glass of amaretto. "Good, or I would have to come and sort you out myself."

He chuckled and patted her hand, but they both knew he would stay true to his values.

When Aziza sat, his mother said, "It's been wonderful meeting you, my dear. I was telling Ryan that he should show you everything off the beaten path."

Aziza responded with a smile and touched his arm. "He's been a great host. I've enjoyed everything so far and I hope he takes your advice."

His mind returned to his surroundings when a man stepped into the passage from a room.

From his relaxed demeanor and colorful clothing, Ryan assumed he was a tourist. They exchanged a smile, and Ryan waited until he went past to slide the key card into the lock.

He was totally focused on Aziza. If he was going to trust her with his whole heart, he had to be sure she would keep her words and promises to him, no matter how difficult the circumstances.

Chapter 27

The suite was in semi-darkness when he entered. In the glow of the lamplight, Sunita was swaddled under several blankets on the sofa bed. He entered the bedroom where Aziza was snoozing while the television played softly in the background.

He leaned over the bed, kissed the curve of her neck, then trailed his tongue over her skin.

Aziza moaned, then rolled over to press her lips to his. As her lids lifted, she asked. "Did you find the girls? Were they all right?"

He sat and unlaced his boots, while sharing some aspects of the visit to *El Zalaam*.

"Poor kids," she said, scooting across the mattress to sit next to him. "I hope things continue to get better for them."

"The Skeihh is a good man. I'm sure they'll be all right. Eventually."

"That's great." She laid a hand on his thigh. "I haven't had dinner. Want me to order room service?"

He nodded. "Something light, like a club sandwich. I need to bathe first."

"Sure, I'll do that in the meantime."

Stroking her cheek, he said, "Thanks, love. We'll talk over dinner."

Aziza's gaze shifted, as if that was the last thing she wanted, but she nodded.

He took his time in the shower, running through the situations he'd encountered in the past few days. Durabia was a beautiful place, but danger lurked around the unsuspecting, as with many other places on earth. But he couldn't picture himself anywhere else since Aziza was here.

His return to the bedroom coincided with the arrival of the food. He pulled on a pair of sweat pants and a tee-shirt and padded into the living room where Aziza, who was dressed identically, met him in front of the sofa and slid both arms around him. She buried her face in his chest, inhaled deeply, then led him to the table where he drew out a chair for her. When she sat, he slid into the seat next to her.

They ate their sandwiches in silence and drank fruit juice. Finally, Ryan laid his napkin on the table and placed one hand on top of Aziza's. "It's time for us to talk."

A half-smile lifted one side of her mouth while she piled their plates together and covered them. "Do we have to?"

"Yes, we do. Let's go to the bedroom where we won't disturb Sunita."

Her sigh was heavy, but she allowed him to guide her into the room. They stood face to face next to the bed, studying each other in silence. Sliding both hands into his pockets, Ryan said, "You made a promise to me, so you heard when I said you were *not* to leave this suite. Where did you go?"

Arms folded, she declared, "Sunita and I went to lunch."

"And?" Ryan raised both eyebrows. "Room service wasn't good enough?"

"That's not it." Aziza tipped her chin up as she slipped into defense mode. "I went to the personnel department."

"Why?"

"They wanted to see me." She pointed over her shoulder. "The HR Director called."

"I'm listening." He didn't touch her, but tilted his head to one side, waiting.

Aziza's shifting gaze revealed her discomfort. She knew she'd crossed a line. "I went to my apartment."

"*Your apartment?*" Ryan massaged his forehead and sighed. The woman he loved more than anything else had no sense of self-preservation. "I'm still waiting for the rest of it. You know ... the part where Akbar chased you."

"I promised I wouldn't leave, but—"

He stepped into her space, forcing Aziza to back up. "If I knew all the ends of this case were tied up, I would have told you so. But since I didn't, I trusted you to keep your word."

When he looked beyond her, Aziza turned to see what captured his attention.

Sunita stood in the doorway, rubbing the sleep from her eyes. Her worried gaze slid between them, as if she feared the two adults would come to blows.

"It's okay, sweetie. Go back to bed, we're just talking," Aziza said, turning sideways. "We'll keep our voices down."

While she spoke Aziza wore a reassuring smile, which fell away when Sunita moved out of range.

Ryan rubbed his jaw, which was itchy. His beard needed tending. "After promising me you would stay here, you left without even a note to say you were going out. I'm definitely not okay with that. D'you know the places my mind went to when I came back and you weren't here?" He waved one hand to encompass the space around them. "The only reason I didn't start tearing this hotel apart was the fact that the room didn't look as if someone dragged you out of it."

Aziza flinched, then murmured, "I'm sorry."

As his skin heated, he inhaled to calm himself. "I didn't ask you to stay here because I wanted to restrict your movements. I wanted you here with me because I care about you." He brushed past Aziza, walked to the sliding door, and stared into the darkness. The blackness of the sky would be nothing compared to what life would look like if she hadn't survived. When he faced her and spoke, his voice was husky.

"In case I haven't made it plain to you, woman, I love the very ground you walk on. If anything happened to you, I do not know how I would make it without you."

As she approached him, he kept talking. "Dropping everything and coming halfway around the world to find you must be a clue to how I feel about you, Aziza Hampton."

She rested both hands on his chest, then slid them around his neck. After kissing his chin softly, she said, "Forgive me?"

He let out a heavy breath. "Yeah, when I'm done ranting at you." With both hands, she pulled his head down and brushed his lips with hers, then rained soft kisses over his cheeks and jaw. "How about now?"

"That's unfair, but I suppose you know that." He stroked her cheeks with his thumbs. "Despite all of that, if you've made any plans, whatever they are, you need to change them."

"I beg your pardon?" The penitent expression that took over her face disappeared as Aziza's head reared back.

He took his time caressing her features with his gaze while his hands descended to her hips. "Seeing that I can't trust you to be where you say you're going to be, I need you where I'm sure you'll be safe."

"And where might that be?" she asked, her tone cautious.

"By my side, of course." He pulled her in close, sank his teeth gently into her earlobe, then soothed it with a kiss. "Aziza Hampton, will you marry me?"

She pushed against his chest and leaned away so she could see his face. "Are you serious?"

Ryan sank one hand into her hair and nuzzled the skin behind her ear. "Why on earth would you think I'm joking at a time like this?"

"Because it's so unexpected?" She gasped, then moaned when the tip of his tongue stroked her skin.

"I agree that life is full of surprises." He pressed his lips to hers, claiming her mouth while he fused her body against his. He raised his head to stare into Aziza's glazed eyes. Instead of giving in to his need, he forced his mind back to settling certain matters between them.

"The one thing I learned after you left Paradise Island was that we should seize the moment."

"What do you mean, specifically?" Aziza asked.

"I'll show you in a minute." He guided her to sit on the end of the mattress, then went to the closet where he opened the safe and removed the ring.

Curiosity filled her eyes as he approached with his hands hidden behind him.

Ryan prodded her thighs apart and kneeled between her legs. He hugged her around the waist, pressing his head to her chest and breathing in the scent of jasmine and lemon. A familiar aroma from her favourite perfume.

Looking deep into her eyes, he prepared to get his words in the right order. "Aziza Hampton, will you do me the honor of marrying me, staying by my side, having my kids ... " his lips curved in a grin, "and generally being where you say you're going to be when you say you're going to be there?"

Her lips twitched and for a second he thought she was going to laugh, then her eyes went liquid and she hugged him, kissing his forehead and cheeks. Aziza sniffed, then cleared her throat. "I don't know about always being where I should be one hundred percent of the time but, of course, I'll be your wife."

Ryan wanted to jump up and roar, like he did at football matches when his team was winning, but the thought of frightening the child in the next room stopped him. He released the happiness bubbling inside him by grinning wide and hugging Aziza. "Say no more, my love."

He opened the jewelry box, removed the ring, and slid it on her finger.

While Aziza studied the diamond, he brushed a tear from her cheek.

"Did you come prepared or what?" She rested both hands on his shoulders as she looked deep into his eyes. "How did you know you would find me?"

"I came to do what I should have done the last time we were together, and I wasn't about to be denied."

"So, why didn't you ask me then?" she said softly, massaging his shoulder muscles.

"I was being a fool, I guess, thinking we had all the time in the world when I could have lost the best thing in my life."

While her agile fingers eased the tension from his shoulders, Aziza asked, "So you're saying if I wanted to keep my job, I don't have a choice?"

He chuckled. "I'm not saying any such thing, but the one thing I know is that wherever I go, you go."

She cupped his face and delivered a steamy kiss, swirling her tongue around his and making him want to undress her. When she pulled away, Aziza wouldn't look at him, as if she was keeping a secret. He gripped her around the waist, moving his thumbs back and forth. "How about you cough up whatever is bothering you?"

"There's something I want to ask you." She stroked his beard with gentle fingers. "It's about Sunita, but it will keep for now."

Chapter 28

"I chewed her out for not keeping her promise, but Akbar chasing down Aziza helped us." Ryan glanced at the men in the room and those linked by satellite. "Things could have turned out differently for her if he had a mind to harm her in that room."

This Monday morning found them deep in a brainstorming and wrap-up session inside Khalil's headquarters. They sat around a horseshoe conference table that faced the massive screen, which was segmented among the Kings participating via satellite.

"True." Daron spun his hat before setting it on the table. "He was the last piece to the puzzle that none of the other guys spoke about, although he was the cornerstone of their business."

Dro grinned, "I guess you could say there is indeed some kind of honor among thieves."

"Not when you dig deeper under the surface." Khalil chuckled. "Nobody mentioned him because they felt they had a leg up on you by withholding information."

"That sounds right," Bashir said. "They knew it was possible that you wouldn't make the connection since his role wasn't obvious."

"Right." Ryan tapped his notes. "If women were missing from the hotel willy-nilly, someone would have eventually made the connection."

Bashir stroked his beard, frowning. "I do not understand this term willy-nilly."

"It means random or haphazard."

He raised one brow. "Haphazard?"

"Oh, boy," Ryan said, "Think about it like—"

"The way Ryan wanted to forget the niceties and beat up the bartender because he knew the location of the women and chose not to tell us," Dro explained.

"You're wrong for that," Ryan said, as the others, including Bashir, laughed.

When Shaz stopped grinning, he said, "My cousin has always been a hot-blooded rabble-rouser. I remember the time when—"

Ryan cut him off with a glare. "This meeting is not the forum for family jokes."

Still grinning, Shaz held up both hands. "You win, but at some point we will adjourn this meeting. At that time … "

Ryan gave him another quelling look. "So like I was saying, Akbar had a hand in selecting victims from among the hotel staff and guests. He was smart, too." After a glance at the file in front of him, Ryan continued, "In the five years he's been at the hotel, just under fifty women have gone missing. Calvin, Daron, and Nicco have been through the surveillance tapes provided by the hotel, which covered the timelines in which they disappeared. He was in contact with all of them, and every one disappeared from Encounters."

The tapes, which Daron had cut and spooled together, played on one side of the screen. Each slide supported Ryan's statement.

Sheikh Kamran broke his silence. "Does this mean that the police have all the parties involved in custody?"

"Most of them. Aside from submitting a report on the arrests that resulted from our efforts, the police haven't done much of anything. Ryan shot an amused glance in Dro's direction. "They picked up Akbar this morning, as well as the man who invaded my room."

The police chief and his assistant had been invited to this meeting and entered the room at the Sheik's bidding. They approached as if walking on eggshells and stopped shy of the table.

The Sheikh did not invite them to sit.

Ryan's gaze went to the assistant commissioner. "I have my suspicious about who sent him, but anyway, the bartender and his partner in crime are under arrest. We established that the container driver and his assistant were not involved, but the owner of the plant has been held without bail."

The police commissioner cleared his throat and shifted from one foot to the other. "Greetings. We owe you gentlemen for your help in bringing two sets of criminals to justice."

The Sheikh held up one hand and growled, "Silence. From the beginning, the two of you were given the opportunity to carry out the roles you were entrusted with, but you failed miserably. Aside from the loss of your pension, you can be sure charges will be brought against you for negligence."

The men quailed under his words.

Then Sheikh Kamran turned his attention to Jai. "Who are we missing in this equation?"

Ryan focused on Jai, who sipped from a glass of water, then said, "The business of organ harvesting and human trafficking is lucrative. It extends from the lowest levels of society to the highest. There's a little girl under Aziza and Ryan's care who inadvertently helped us crack this case."

No one moved as they waited for him to continue.

He recounted Sunita's history and as his words dropped, Ryan thought the term 'deafening silence' was apt. Not even the men attending the meeting via The Castle's secure satellite system moved a muscle.

Jai explained the role of *El Zalaam* and added that despite the nationals' protest, the place had been shuttered.

The two officers shifted on their feet, as if they thought the other men would blame them for *El Zalaam's* existence, but everyone understood it was an unsavoury and long-standing part of Durabia's culture that needed to change.

"Sunita was hysterical when she saw a certain doctor at the clinic," Ryan said. He scanned the men's faces, then added, "You know the rest of that story."

Chaz and Jai exchanged an uncomfortable glance that Ryan understood. Jai still felt some kind of way about being associated in any way with that deviant, through no fault of his own.

"Although I fired Dr. Butala on the spot, we kept tabs on him, knowing that in his panic he would try to cover his ass." Jai tipped his head toward Daron. "Not only did he like little girls, he was one of two masterminds involved in organ harvesting. His surgery was set up in the belly of that meat-packing plant. We suspect they were shipping out the women in the delivery truck, *before taking their organs*, because they knew we were on their trail. Not only did they trade in murder, but also misery. Misery for the women who had to live with being sold into slavery."

The officers looked at each other, then stood at attention.

"The thing is," Daron said, looking directly at the Assistant Commissioner. "To facilitate certain procedures and get through roadblocks and across borders, they needed official help."

"Like the kind provided by the police," Sheikh Kamran said, placing a narrow-eyed gaze on the officers.

The former Commissioner balked, as if outraged by the accusation.

His portly assistant sprouted beads of sweat on his forehead and lowered his head.

The Sheikh shot to his feet, and his voice thundered through the room. "Please do not tell me that the organization meant to protect our citizens has facilitated this criminal activity."

Again a lull fell over the room.

Then Dro said, "It is not as bad as you think."

The Sheikh sat, still focused on the officers. "Please, continue."

"Only one of your commissioners is involved." His gaze shifted to the man who now dabbed his forehead with a handkerchief. "From

Daron's spyware, we have established that Dr. Butala and Assistant Commissioner Handal know each other and are in business together."

"This is not true!" Officer Handal shouted, only to lapse into silence when the screen came to life. He stood talking to Dr. Butala with a small igloo between them. Several others had already been loaded into an SUV. The doctor flipped open the cover and although the container with the body part was shrouded in ice, Angela had translated their conversation relating how the harvesting had been done.

At that point in the film, the policeman had reassured the doctor that the escort was waiting to transport the remainder of the body and the harvested organs across the border into Nadaum. With the evidence disposed of, no one in Durabia would be any wiser.

Daron lips quirked in approval. Before the arrival of the officers, he revealed that Angela and Nicco had spent the rest of their time in Durabia shadowing Dr. Butala at Jai's request. Their diligence had paid big dividends.

"You should be ashamed of yourself," Sheikh Kamran said. "I promise you, you will be punished to the fullest extent of the law."

Officer Handal dashed to the door and disappeared before any of them could move.

None of them chased him.

He reappeared a few seconds later, escorted by Nicco, who asked, "Going somewhere?"

"Like a speeding bullet, no less." Ryan chuckled at his joke.

His smile vanished when the Skeikh asked, "Do we know how and why they chose the women?"

"I'd say they did their selection based on observation and using the opportunities presented to them," Ryan said.

The Skeikh and the former Commissioner glared at the shorter man, whose attention was fixed on his shoes.

"I'll hold these two until you make transportation arrangements," Nicco said to the Sheikh, who leaned toward his assistant.

The attaché got to his feet while Sheikh Kamran turned his steely gaze on the Commissioner. "Get out. You are a disgrace to your uniform, and to the Durabia Constabulary Force."

He opened his mouth, but one look from the Sheikh had him moving toward the door in Nicco's firm grip. The Sheik's assistant followed them and closed the door.

In an inclusive gesture, the Sheikh opened his hands toward the men at the table and those on screen. "I would like to thank the Kings and Knights for their good work. There are more tentacles to sever, but we have to find them first. You cut one off and another replaces it in a short time." His gaze settled on Ryan. "In view of your part in this case, I'm asking that you think about staying in Durabia. It is my intention to set up a permanent task force to eliminate this scourge, which is part of the underbelly of Middle Eastern countries. With help from the Kings, I am certain you can do more good."

The offer surprised Ryan and left him speechless. When he recovered, he said, "What I've seen of the country, I like, but if I want to stay alive, I'd better discuss this with my fiancée before saying yes or no."

The room erupted in laughter. When their merriment subsided, Ryan sent a sideways glance at Bashir. "I want to thank Bashir for his dedication to duty. He stuck with us every step of the way. Sometimes, I didn't trust him, but I know he's one of the good guys."

Bashir acknowledged his thanks with a nod.

"He can be the first member of your task force if you say yes," the Skeikh commented. "I would also like Hassan and Rahm to be part of that unit."

The strapping man saluted him across the table and Ryan bobbed his head in return.

"I will graciously accept that offer if I can make staying in Durabia a reality. There is one more item I would like to mention before we close," Ryan said. "Aziza has fallen in love with Sunita, and I have, too. Sunita feels the same way about Aziza. Is there a way we can become foster parents to her and eventually adopt her?"

The Sheikh considered that for a moment. "If I read the details correctly, her family sold her to a businessman in *El Zalaam*. Since that is the case, it is unlikely her parents will welcome her back. If we send her home, they will only sell her again, or she may face a worse fate.

"I would like my wife to speak with Sunita to ensure this is what she wants. After they talk, I will contact the social services division of our government and make that happen. It is the least I can do to thank you for your service to Durabia."

Ryan smiled, relieved that he had good news for Aziza. "Thank you."

Weeks ago, Ryan would have thought it impossible for him to become a ready-made father. He was neither prepared nor willing, but this was his new situation and he'd do anything in his power to keep Aziza and Sunita happy.

"If there is no other business on the agenda," Khalil said, "could someone move for the adjournment of this meeting?"

All the men shouted a resounding, "Aye."

Chapter 29

Aziza didn't think it was possible to love Ryan more than she had a day, hour, minute, or second ago. But it was.

They stood in the gardens of the royal palace in the middle of a fairy-tale wedding. Ryan was handsome and debonair in a white suit, paired with a navy shirt and white silk tie.

Shaz stood by his side, dressed similarly. He had flown in for a director's meeting with the Kings of the Castle, and according to him their wedding was the icing on the cake.

Aziza was delighted to see his wife and their daughter, who represented home. An obviously pregnant and radiant Camilla made Aziza's mind veer off to what she would look like in the same state, and how soon that might happen.

They spent another week in Durabia. Much of the time, Aziza was in the company of the Royals—the Sheikh's wife and her niece, Blair—organizing their wedding. Once Ryan floated the idea of them marrying in Durabia, the Royals were on board, putting every aspect in place in the shortest possible time. For Ryan's part in the rescue, they insisted on footing the bill for the wedding.

Aziza spent the rest of her time at the crisis center with Amanda's team. They worked feverishly to reunite the women she had been confined with, with their families. Some cases were more challenging, as their families had sold them. Those individuals opted to stay in Durabia, if they could find jobs and shelter.

Rae and Linda, both colleagues of Amanda, dedicated themselves to making that happen.

The way Ryan had explained their extended stay was that he and the Kings were closing the assignment given by the Sheikh. He also insisted that it made sense for them to get married now, since there wouldn't be a better opportunity. They conversed for days about how they would divide their time. When they left Durabia, she would return to Paradise Island with him. They still had to make plans to accommodate Sunita, who was burrowing deeper into Aziza's heart by the day.

Ryan asked Aziza's parents for permission to marry her via a video call and promised they would also have a reception in Evanston. Now, both families viewed their wedding via the Internet.

Aziza stopped musing when Khalil Germaine Maharaj spoke in his quiet but authoritative voice. "I understand you have written vows for each other."

Ryan smoothed the back of Aziza's hand with his thumb. "Yes, we have."

While the breeze ruffled the white hair at his widow's peak, Khalil said, "Please, speak your hearts to each other."

Ryan faced her, and joined their hands. The affection in his gaze made her feel as if she was the only woman in the world.

"Aziza Mariah Hampton, from day one you made an impact that no one could erase. Time and distance have affected us for years, but having you forever means it's been well worth the wait."

His earnest confession brought tears to her eyes as a few "Aaaawws" came from their guests.

"No matter where you go in this world, I'll be by your side. I promise to love and cherish you until death separates us."

Aziza tipped her head back to avoid smearing her makeup and breathed through her mouth to prevent an undignified sniffle.

"Dorian Emory Bostwick, I didn't know what it meant to be in love until I met you," she said, "You've taught me how to love selflessly, to act for the higher good of our loved ones, and to function as part of a team. My experience in Durabia has taught me that you're a keeper." At this point she chuckled. "I'm giving you fair warning that you're never getting rid of me."

Khalil and those around them laughed after her declaration.

With her fingers, Aziza caressed his palms. "Thank you for loving me, even when I drive you to distraction."

She could have sworn his eyes were moist, but Ryan cleared his throat and leaned toward her, his intention clear.

"No, sir," Khalil moved one finger back and forth. "Just one more moment. By the power vested in me by the City of Chicago, and the country of Durabia, I declare you man and wife."

With an indulgent smile, he said, "You may now kiss the bride."

Ryan lifted her veil, and his hands settled on her waist as their lips met. The hunger in his kiss was enough for Aziza to forget where they stood. When her arms encircled his neck, a familiar voice intruded on their passion.

"Leave some for later," Shaz said, "The longer you keep this up, the less time we'll have to eat."

Ryan cut his cousin a bad look. "All you think about is food, and there's no evidence of where you're putting it."

"Mind ya business," Shaz shot back, "and while you're at it, be thankful you're not the one feeding me."

A wave of laughter rose among the guests, which included a few Kings.

After she threw the bouquet, which one of the Sheikh's female relatives caught, they left the gazebo that was decorated with a cloud of white roses and baby's breath.

Sunita walked ahead of them, swinging the empty basket at her side. She had made a beautiful flower girl with her hair braided into a corona and threaded with miniature white roses.

Her future worried Aziza, but she put it to the back of her mind for now, confident that her situation would work out for the best. At the garden's entrance, she exchanged a kiss with Ryan before the men got his attention.

They surrounded him, giving congratulatory hugs and advice about marriage.

Julene and Naima escorted Aziza back to the room in the palace where she had dressed for the wedding. Sunita shadowed them, still hanging on to the basket where she sat on a loveseat across the room.

Aziza stood in front of the mirror admiring the dress that had been crafted for her in less than a week. The lace-and-embroidery creation enhanced her curves and gave her the aura of a queen.

"Thank you for inviting me," Julene gushed, while helping Aziza out of the dress.

"Me, too," Naima said. "I have not attended a wedding in a long time. I am honored to be part of yours, especially after the way you helped me."

"You both did me a favor," Aziza said. "If you didn't come, there wouldn't have been anybody in attendance for me. In the flesh, that is."

Aziza winked at Sunita. "You did a great job, sweetie."

"I was happy to help, Auntie."

In the past week, Aziza had conversed with Sunita to build her skills at English. Her confidence level had also risen, and she was more relaxed in Ryan's presence.

Under Naima's instruction, Aziza sat in front of the mirror. With deft touches, Naima repaired her makeup. Then, Julene neatened Aziza's hair that she'd tamed earlier with a flatiron and holding gel.

After Julene groomed every stray hair back in place, Aziza slipped into a cream dress with a matching jacket. She ran a finger over the silky petal of the rose she had removed from her bouquet, then held it to her nose and inhaled deeply. The fragrance reminded her of the goodness of life and its many simple blessings.

She hugged Naima, who had been a constant companion during the last week. She was currently in the shelter, but had decided to return to Senegal. Aziza wasn't sure when she'd see her again, if ever, but they had promised to stay in touch.

The three women descended the stairs and entered the ballroom where some guests sat and others stood around talking with champagne glasses in hand.

The Sheikh and Sheikha sat at a table on a raised dais and were soon joined by Amanda, Hassan, Khalil, Chaz, and Blair, as well as other distinguished-looking guests she assumed were part of the royal family.

Ryan appeared at Aziza's side and escorted her to another table set for them and the wedding party.

The official portion of the reception did not take long. Khalil acted as the Master of Ceremonies and those who spoke, including Shaz, kept their good wishes and tributes tight and humorous.

At the end of a meal that included a fig salad with blackberries, creamy hummus, and spiced lamb with pine nuts, topped off by a pomegranate gravita and pistachio baklava. To honour their foreign guests, the caterers also prepared an American menu.

When most of the food was consumed, Khalil tapped a wine glass with a knife to get everybody's attention. The room went quiet when he stood.

"I do not want to steal Ryan and Aziza's thunder," he said, "but there is no better time to do this."

Gesturing to Ryan, he continued, "Mr Bostwick, would you stand, please?"

Ryan seemed mystified, but he did what Khalil asked and stood next to him at the glass podium.

"The Kings of the Castle believe in highlighting good when it is done and encourage service at the highest level."

The only sound in their elegant surroundings was the random clink of cutlery and the piped music playing at a low setting.

"For his part in rescuing the kidnapped women a week ago, and uncovering the source of a criminal enterprise, it is my pleasure to name Dorian "Ryan" Emory Bostwick, the Knight of Paradise Island."

A delighted grin covered Ryan's face as he accepted a gold figure of a knight on an oval pedestal. Khalil also handed him a small box, which Ryan guessed contained cufflinks like the ones the other Knights wore. "The Kings are impressed with your initiative and skills." Khalil chuckled, then continued, "Even if you *are* hot-headed, like someone else we could mention, but will not."

"Thank you. All the women involved can thank Aziza." Ryan's gaze settled on her. "When Shaz told me she'd been kidnapped, it was as if my heart had been ripped out. There was nothing I could do other than fight to get it back."

He returned to their table with the backdrop of rousing applause. When he sat, Aziza cupped his cheek. "I'm so proud of you, babe." Eyes closed, he kissed her palm.

The reception continued for another hour before they left for their suite.

On her way out of the ballroom, Aziza stopped at the children's table. Last night she had explained to Sunita that she would be staying at the palace while she and Ryan celebrated their honeymoon.

Sunita's anxiety was heart-breaking to watch, but now as she kissed her cheek, Sunita seemed more at ease.

"If you need anything at all," Aziza reminded her, "ask an adult to get me on the phone. I'll call you in the morning."

One child, a girl slightly younger than Sunita, linked an arm through hers. "She will be fine, Auntie. We will take care of her. Right, Sunita?"

To Aziza's surprise, Sunita nodded. "I will be okay."

The chauffeured ride back to the hotel took ten minutes, and the moment Ryan lifter her over the threshold of the suite, he removed each item of her clothing a piece at a time. When she lay nude before his eyes, Ryan worshiped every part of her body until she squirmed on the mattress, begging him to take her.

Their coupling was hot and frantic with need. They had agreed to wait until they were married before consummating their union, and with Sunita in the suite, abstaining made sense. Each night, they slept with the bedroom door open, in case she woke and needed Aziza.

The next time Ryan brought her to ecstasy, Aziza yelled his name and clung to him as if she couldn't survive without his touch. As sleep overcame her, Ryan whispered, "Mrs. Bostwick, there's more gas left in this engine."

She stretched and shifted to face him. With a mischievous smile teasing her lips, she said, "I know a way we can move the needle to empty."

Chapter 30

Three glorious days and two nights with Ryan mellowed Aziza. After a dinner of Mansaf, comprising lamb, yogurt, and rice, for Aziza and Ryan and a hamburger and fries for Sunita, they sat in the living area of the suite having dessert. The bite-sized servings of Kanafeh, a soft cheese pastry covered in syrup, took a little getting used to, but Aziza enjoyed every bite. Ryan declined, claiming he was stuffed.

After she and Sunita rid their fingers and mouths of the sticky delight, the girl ran back to the living room, dropped one arm around her plump brown bear, and pulled a book into her lap. While she didn't yet trust Ryan one hundred percent, he gave her space, and as the days passed her jumpiness around him subsided.

Aziza forced Ryan to reposition himself on the loveseat so she could lie on his lap. She wriggled around, then settled in one position and sighed. "This is the life," she mumbled. "Now, if Mom and Dad would stop asking when they will see us, everything would be perfect."

Ryan's chest rose and fell as he laughed. He lay the tablet aside and kissed her forehead. "We need to have that talk about our future. The Sheikh made me an offer."

She went still, then raised her head. "How come you're only telling me this now?"

"Sweetheart, a man has to work out things in his head before he can explain it to someone else, especially if it's appealing and he might have to make a case to his wife."

She sat up. "This sounds serious."

After pulling himself upright, Ryan slipped an arm around her and kept his voice pitched low. "Sheikh Kamran asked me to be part of a task force to stem sex trafficking and organ harvesting."

Her heart thudded in slow, painful beats. Although the few weeks had been a wonderful interlude, she'd been living in suspense and simultaneously looking forward to leaving Durabia. Now, Ryan was telling her something different.

"That sounds like staying here indefinitely," she mumbled.

He pressed a kiss to her temple. "I was thinking about it, but if you don't want to be here, I understand. In any case, I have to return home. Myles and I have a big project on the horizon, and we need to plan for the future if I'm going to be in Durabia."

Aziza poked him in the chest. "You didn't even know if you'd find me, so that that tells me you planned to be here for however long it took."

"You got that right." He slid one hand down to her waist. "But let's talk about it before we say no. I believe you'd be a great asset in terms of sharing your experience with other women, letting them know there's hope. In fact, we could even develop a self-defense course, teaching women how to protect themselves both physically and mentally."

She rubbed her cheek against his jaw. "You've put some thought into it already, huh?"

Slowly, Ryan nodded. "It would be something new and different for me. Myles can easily handle my end of the business by hiring someone to fulfil my role for the jobs on the ground. You would be safe since we'd be working together most of the time, but I know you can take care of yourself. We'd only have to upgrade your self-defense and coaching skills."

"Like I said, you have it all figured out." The thought of her family made her sigh.

"What's the problem?" he asked.

"My family. I need to see them. Skype and Zoom are not the same as person-to-person contact."

"Agreed. When we leave here, we'll go straight to Evanston so Miss Constance can see that I brought her baby girl home in all her perfection. And since I don't want your father to send out a search party for me ... "

His hand climbed and settled under her breast, kneading with gentle pressure.

Aziza sent a pointed look at Sunita. "Don't start what you can't finish, Mr. Bostwick."

"Awww, shucks." He laughed, then spoke next to her ear. "Should we talk to her now? Tell her what's up?"

With an affectionate gaze focused on Sunita, Aziza said, "I don't see why not."

She leaned away from Ryan, but joined her hand with his. "Sunita, honey, we want to talk with you for a minute."

The child dragged her attention from the open book and edged sideways on the sofa to face them.

"Did you enjoy your time in the palace over the weekend?" Aziza asked.

Sunita squeezed the bear to her chest. "Yes, I like the children there."

"And you like Durabia?"

That dampened Sunita's mood, but she looked directly at Ryan, then answered, "*Not El Zalaam.*"

"We understand that, sweetie."

Ryan's leg tensed against hers. It was clear Sunita still thought all men were bad people. That was something they agreed to work on, along with planning for Sunita's schooling.

"Do you know what adoption is?" Aziza asked.

"No."

"It's when a child gets to live with a mother and a father who takes care of them."

Sunita considered that, throwing shy glances at them.

Squeezing Ryan's hand, Aziza said, "Ryan and I want to do that for you, be your mother and father."

When she didn't respond, Aziza said, "Would you like that?"

The little girl stared at the blank television screen as if she were the only one in the room.

"Sunita?"

She still didn't move.

Aziza rose and sat next to her, with an arm around her thin shoulders. "It's okay if you want to think about it for a while."

Sunita shook her head so violently a bloom fell from her hair. She'd been so ecstatic with having her hair braided for the wedding, one of the adults at the palace re-did it in the same style, complete with miniature roses. With tears streaming down her face, she leaned against Aziza.

Instead of soothing Sunita, Aziza's comforting words had the opposite effect. She cried as if someone had died, but when Aziza attempted to move out of her hold, Sunita's arms tightened around her. All Aziza could do was stroke her hair and allow her to empty herself.

Aziza sensed Ryan's helplessness, but there was nothing he could do. Seconds later, he got to his feet and went to the bedroom. He reappeared with a handful of facial tissue, which he gave to Aziza, then returned to the loveseat.

The minutes slipped by until Sunita was calm enough for Aziza to continue their conversation.

"Sweetie, do you understand what we are asking you?"

"Yes, Auntie."

"Do you want us to be your parents? We'd love to have you."

"That would make me very happy," she said, wiping tears from her cheeks. She caught her breath, then added, "Are we leaving Durabia?"

"Ryan and I will have to go to America to see my family. Then we have to visit his home on Paradise Island, before we come back to Durabia."

Sunita blew her nose, then asked, "I am coming with you to those places?"

"The answer is yes, if you would like to travel with us. If you don't trust us enough yet, we can ask that you stay in the palace until we return."

She answered without hesitation. "No, I would like to come with you."

"That's settled then."

"How soon will we leave?" Excitement colored Sunita's voice as her eyes sparkled.

Aziza looked at Ryan, who said, "We'll be here for as long as it takes to get a passport for Sunita and a visa, if necessary, so she can travel."

Hugging Sunita, Aziza said, "I'm excited about going home. We'll have to do some more shopping to get you ready for the trip."

Aziza removed the used tissues from Sunita's hand and handed then to Ryan, who left the room. When he returned, Sunita smiled at him. "Thank you."

"You're welcome," he said.

Assured that Sunita felt better and was back to exploring her book, Aziza tugged Ryan's hand and walked him to the balcony. She stood in his embrace as evening turned to night and the calm river glinted below. The city lights flickered on as darkness fell, sealing them in a cocoon of contentment. Her heart was full, and her gratitude spilled from her lips, "Father God, we want to thank You for everything You've done for us and the gift of a daughter You've given us. Help us to continue to look up to You for help as we navigate the beginning of the rest of our lives. We give You thanks and praise."

Ryan joined her in a resounding "Amen."

"Sounds to me like you've decided what we're doing," he said, as she turned to face the starry sky.

She moved the back of her head against his chest. "You kinda led the way by telling me your plans."

"They weren't final before you approved them." He chuckled and turned her to face him. "I'm no fool. My mama raised me right."

Aziza slid both arms around his neck as love for him stole her breath.

"Thing is, Ryan, you've ruined me for anyone else, so wherever you go, I go."

His teeth flashed in a wide grin. "So, you love me like that, huh?"

"Don't go getting big-headed. You love me the same." Laughter spilled from her lips as her hands slid down to his chest. "I'd go even further and say you adore me."

He rained kisses on her forehead and sealed her in his arms as if he had no intention of releasing her. With his lips nuzzling her ear, he whispered, "I do, Mrs. Bostwick. I do."

About the *Knights of the Castle* Series

Don't miss the hot new standalone series. The Kings of the Castle made them family, but the Knights will transform the world.

Book 1 - King of Durabia – Naleighna Kai

No good deed goes unpunished, or that's how Ellena Kiley feels after she rescues a child and the former Crown Prince of Durabia offers to marry her.

Kamran learns of a nefarious plot to undermine his position with the Sheikh and jeopardize his ascent to the throne. He's unsure how Ellena, the fiery American seductress, fits into the plan but she's a secret weapon he's unwilling to relinquish.

Ellena is considered a sister by the Kings of the Castle and her connection to Kamran challenges her ideals, her freedoms, and her heart. Plus, loving him makes her a potential target for his enemies. When Ellena is kidnapped, Kamran is forced to bring in the Kings.

In the race against time to rescue his woman and defeat his enemies, the kingdom of Durabia will never be the same.

Book 2 - Knight of Bronzeville – Naleighna Kai and Stephanie M. Freeman

Chaz Maharaj thought he could maintain the lie of a perfect marriage for his adoring fans … until he met Amanda.

The connection between them should have ended with that unconditional "hall pass" which led to one night of unbridled passion. But once would never satisfy his hunger for a woman who could never be his. When Amanda walked out of his life, it was supposed to be forever. Neither of them could have anticipated fate's plan.

Chaz wants to explore his feelings for Amanda, but Susan has other ideas. Prepared to fight for his budding romance and navigate a plot that's been laid to crush them, an unexpected twist threatens his love and her life.

When Amanda's past comes back to haunt them, Chaz enlists the Kings of the Castle to save his newfound love in a daring escape.

Book 3 - Knight of South Holland – Karen D. Bradley

He's a brilliant inventor, but he'll decimate anyone who threatens his woman.

When the Kings of the Castle recommend Calvin Atwood, strategic defense inventor, to create a security shield for the kingdom of Durabia, it's the opportunity of a lifetime. The only problem—it's a two-year assignment and he promised his fiancée they would step away from their dangerous lifestyle and start a family.

Security specialist, Mia Jakob, adores Calvin with all her heart, but his last assignment put both of their lives at risk. She understands how important this new role is to the man she loves, but the thought that he may be avoiding commitment does cross her mind.

Calvin was sure he'd made the best decision for his and Mia's future, until enemies of the state target his invention and his woman. Set on a collision course with hidden foes, this Knight will need the help of the Kings to save both his Queen and the Kingdom of Durabia.

Book 4 - Lady of Jeffrey Manor – J. S. Cole and Naleighna Kai

He's the kingdom's most eligible bachelor. She's a practical woman on temporary assignment.

When surgical nurse, Blair Swanson, departed the American Midwest for an assignment in the Kingdom of Durabia she had no intention of finding love.

As a member of the royal family, Crown Prince Hassan has a responsibility to the throne. A loveless, arranged marriage is his duty, but the courageous American nurse is his desire.

When a dark secret threatens everything Hassan holds dear, how will he fulfill his royal duty and save the lady who holds his heart?

Book 5 - Knight of Grand Crossing – Hiram Shogun Harris, Naleighna Kai, and Anita L. Roseboro

Rahm did time for a crime he didn't commit. Now that he's free, taking care of the three women who supported him on a hellish journey is his priority, but old enemies are waiting in the shadows.

Rahm Fosten's dream life as a Knight of the Castle includes Marilyn Spears, who quiets the injustice of his rough past, but in his absence a new foe has infiltrated his family.

Marilyn Spears waited for many years to have someone like Rahm in her life. Now that he's home, an unexpected twist threatens to rip him away again. As much as she loves him, she's not willing to go where this new drama may lead.

Meanwhile, Rahm's gift to his Aunt Alyssa brings her to Durabia, where she catches the attention of wealthy surgeon, Ahmad Maharaj. Her attendance at a private Bliss event puts her under his watchful eye, but also in the crosshairs of the worst kind of enemy. Definitely the wrong timing for the rest of the challenges Rahm is facing.

While Rahm and Marilyn navigate their romance, a deadly threat has him and the Kings of the Castle primed to keep Marilyn, Alyssa, and his family from falling prey to an adversary out for bloody revenge.

Book 6 - Knight of Paradise Island – J. L. Campbell

Someone is killing women and the villain's next target strikes too close to the Kingdom of Durabia.

Dorian "Ryan" Bostwick is a protector and he's one of the best in the business. When a King of the Castle assigns him to find his former lover, Aziza, he stumbles upon a deadly underworld operating close to the Durabian border.

Aziza Hampton had just rekindled her love affair with Ryan when a night out with friends ends in her kidnapping. Alone and scared, she must find a way to escape her captor and reunite with her lover.

In a race against time, Ryan and the Kings of the Castle follow ominous clues into the underbelly of a system designed to take advantage of the vulnerable. Failure isn't an option and Ryan will rain down hell on earth to save the woman of his heart.

Book 7 - Knight of Irondale – J. L Woodson, Naleighna Kai, and Martha Kennerson

Neesha Carpenter is on the run from a stalker ex-boyfriend, so why are the police hot on her trail?

Neesha escaped the madness of her previous relationship only to discover the Chicago Police have named her the prime suspect in her ex's shooting. With her life spinning out of control, she turns to the one man who's the biggest threat to her heart—Christian Vidal, her high school sweetheart.

Christian has always been smitten with Neesha's strength, intelligence and beauty. He offers her safe haven in the kingdom of Durabia and will do whatever it takes to keep her safe, even enlisting the help of the Kings of the Castle.

Neesha and Christian's rekindled flame burns hotter even as her stay in the country places the royal family at odds with the American government.

As mounting evidence points to Neesha's guilt, Christian must ask the hard question … is the woman he loves being framed or did she pull the trigger?

Book 8 - Knight of Birmingham – Lori Hays and MarZe Scott

Single mothers who are eligible for release, have totally disappeared from the Alabama justice system.

Women's advocate, Meghan Turner, has uncovered a disturbing pattern and she's desperate for help. Then her worse nightmare becomes a horrific reality when her friend goes missing under the same mysterious circumstances.

Rory Tannous has spent his life helping society's most vulnerable. When he learns of Meghan's dilemma, he takes it personal. Rory has his own tragic past and he'll utilize every connection, even the King of the Castle, to help this intriguing woman find her friend and the other women.

As Rory and Meghan work together, the attraction grows and so does the danger. The stakes are high and they will have to risk their love and lives to defeat a powerful adversary.

Book 9 - Knight of Penn Quarter – Terri Ann Johnson and Michele Sims

Following an undercover FBI sting operation that didn't go as planned, Agent Mateo Lopez is ready to put the government agency in his rearview mirror.

A confirmed workaholic, his career soared at the cost of his love life which had crashed and burned until mutual friends arranged a date with beautiful, sharp-witted, Rachel Jordan, a rising star at a children's social services agency.

Unlucky in love, Rachel has sworn off romantic relationships, but Mateo finds himself falling for her in more ways than one. When trouble brews in one of Rachel's cases, he does everything in his power to keep her safe—even if it means resorting to extreme measures.

Will the choices they make bring them closer together or cost them their lives?

About the Kings of the Castle Series

"Did you miss The Kings of the Castle? "They are so expertly crafted and flow so well between each of the books, it's hard to tell each is crafted by a different author. Very well done!" - Lori H…, Amazon and Goodreads

Each King book 2-9 is a standalone, NO cliffhangers

Book 1 – Kings of the Castle, the introduction to the series and story of King of Wilmette (Vikkas Germaine)

USA TODAY, New York Times, and National Bestselling Authors work together to provide you with a world you'll never want to leave. The Castle.

Fate made them brothers, but protecting the Castle, each other, and the women they love, will make them Kings. Their combined efforts to find the current Castle members responsible for the attempt on their mentor's life, is the beginning of dangerous challenges that will alter the path of their lives forever.

These powerful men, unexpectedly brought together by their pasts and current circumstances, will become a force to be reckoned with.

King of Chatham - Book 2 – London St. Charles

While Mariano "Reno" DeLuca uses his skills and resources to create safe havens for battered women, a surge in criminal activity within the Chatham area threatens the women's anonymity and security. When Zuri, an exotic Tanzanian Princess, arrives seeking refuge from an arranged marriage and its deadly consequences, Reno is now forced to relocate the women in the shelter, fend off unforeseen enemies of The Castle, and endeavor not to lose his heart to the mysterious woman.

King of Evanston - Book 3 - J. L. Campbell

Raised as an immigrant, he knows the heartache of family separation firsthand. His personal goals and business ethics collide when a vulnerable woman stands to lose her baby in an underhanded and profitable scheme crafted by powerful, ruthless businessmen and politicians who have nefarious ties to The Castle. Shaz and the Kings of the Castle collaborate to uproot the dark forces intent on changing the balance of power within The Castle and destroying their mentor. National Bestselling Author, J.L. Campbell presents book 3 in the Kings of the Castle Series, featuring Shaz Bostwick.

King of Devon - Book 4 - Naleighna Kai

When a coma patient becomes pregnant, Jaidev Maharaj's medical facility comes under a government microscope and media scrutiny. In the midst of the investigation, he receives a mysterious call from someone in his past that demands that more of him than he's ever been willing to give and is made aware of a dark family secret that will destroy the people he loves most.

King of Morgan Park - Book 5 - Karen D. Bradley

Two things threaten to destroy several areas of Daron Kincaid's life—the tracking device he developed to locate victims of sex trafficking and an inherited membership in a mysterious outfit called The Castle. The new developments set the stage to dismantle the relationship with a woman who's been trained to make men weak or put them on the other side of the grave. The secrets Daron keeps from Cameron and his inner circle only complicates an already tumultuous situation caused by an FBI sting that brought down his former enemies. Can Daron take on his enemies, manage his secrets and loyalty to the Castle without permanently losing the woman he loves?

King of South Shore - Book 6 - MarZe Scott

Award-winning real estate developer, Kaleb Valentine, is known for turning failing communities into thriving havens in the Metro Detroit area. His plans to rebuild his hometown neighborhood are dereailed with one phone call that puts Kaleb deep in the middle of an intense criminal investigation led by a detective who has a personal vendetta. Now he will have to deal with the ghosts of his past before they kill him.

King of Lincoln Park - Book 7 – Martha Kennerson

Grant Khambrel is a sexy, successful architect with big plans to expand his Texas Company. Unfortunately, a dark secret from his past could destroy it all unless he's willing to betray the man responsible for that success, and the woman who becomes the key to his salvation.

King of Hyde Park - Book 8 -Lisa Dodson

Alejandro "Dro" Reyes has been a "fixer" for as long as he could remember, which makes owning a crisis management company focused on repairing professional reputations the perfect fit. The same could be said of Lola Samuels, who is only vaguely aware of his "true" talents and seems to be oblivious to the growing attraction between them. His company, Vantage Point, is in high demand and business in the Windy City is booming. Until a mysterious call following an attempt on his mentor's life forces him to drop everything and accept a fated position with The Castle. But there's a hidden agenda and unexpected enemy that Alejandro doesn't see coming who threatens his life, his woman, and his throne.

King of Lawndale - Book 9 - Janice M. Allen

Dwayne Harper's passion is giving disadvantaged boys the tools to transform themselves into successful men. Unfortunately, the minute he steps up to take his place among the men he considers brothers, two things stand in his way: a political office that does not want the competition Dwayne's new education system will bring, and a well-connected former member of The Castle who will use everything in his power—even those who Dwayne mentors—to shut him down.

J. L. Campbell

National Bestselling Author, J.L. Campbell writes contemporary, paranormal, and sweet romance, romantic suspense, women's fiction, as well as new and young adult novels.

Campbell, who features Jamaican culture in her stories, has penned over thirty books. She is a certified editor, who also writes non-fiction. When she's not writing, Campbell adds to her extensive collection of photos detailing Jamaica's flora and fauna. Visit her on the web at www. joylcampbell.com

Author Profile links:
FB Fan Page - https://www.facebook.com/jlcampbellwrites/
BookBub - https://www.bookbub.com/authors/j-l-campbell
Amazon - amazon.com/author/jlcampbell
Twitter - https://twitter.com/JL_Campbell
Instagram - https://www.instagram.com/jl.campbell/
Newsletter - bit.ly/JLCampbellsNewsletter
GoodReads - https//www.goodreads.com/jlcampbell
Pinterest - https://www.pinterest.com/thewriterssuite

Other Books by J.L. Campbell

Romantic Suspense
Anya's Wish (novella)
Chasing Anya
Contraband
Taming Celeste
Grudge
Hardware
King of Evanston

New Adult
Perfection
Fixation
Persuasion

Women's Fiction
A Baker's Dozen-13 Steps to Distraction (novella)
Dissolution
Distraction
Retribution
Absolution
The Thick of Things
The Heart of Things
The Pain of Things

Young Adult
Christine's Odyssey
Saving Sam

Short Story Collections
Don't Get Mad...Get Even (free)
Don't Get Mad...Get Even: Kicked to the Kerb

Sweet Romance
The Vet's Christmas Pet
The Vet's Valentine Gift
The Vet's Secret Wish
Cupid's Gift
Sold! (Relative Ties Book 1)
Blindsided (Relative Ties Book 2)

Contemporary Romance
The Short Game (Par-For-The-Course) Book 1
The Long Game (Par-For-The-Course) Book 2
The Blind Shot (Par-For-The-Course) Book 3
Forever Mine
The Spice of Life

Paranormal Romance
Phantasm